New Love, Spilt Milk, and Potbellied Pigs

New Love,
Spilt Milk, and
Potbellied Pigs

Thomas Fish & Jillian Ober

Book Design & Production: Columbus Publishing Lab
www.ColumbusPublishingLab.com

Original photography by Sarah Henderson
Stock photography sourced from iStock, Pixabay, and Morguefile

LCCN: 2018963085
Paperback ISBN: 978-1-63337-234-4
E-book ISBN: 978-1-63337-241-2

Printed in the United States of America
1 3 5 7 9 10 8 6 4 2

This book is dedicated to the GLOW Foundation

and the Woodward family.

Table of Contents

Acknowledgments

Next Chapter Book Club members, facilitators, coordinators, and affiliates around the world served as the inspiration for this book. Their enjoyment of and positive experiences with the book clubs made our work a labor of love.

This book would not have been possible without the generous encouragement and financial support from the GLOW Foundation. They provided the resources to develop, print, market, and disseminate *New Love*. In particular, Robert Woodward has been an amazing advocate for this project. Thanks so much, Bob!

We express sincere appreciation to Marta Csejtey, who assisted with writing a number of the pieces in this book, including "A Walk with Randy," "Mr. Tell Everything," and "What's up with the Potbellied Pig?". Marta provided significant creativity and insight throughout the writing process.

i

We are extremely grateful to Columbus Publishing Lab and editor Emily Hitchcock. Emily has been a guiding force since we decided to publish this book. Her calm professionalism and reliability, combined with her creative and technical expertise, made working with her a delight. We knew we could count on Emily, and were not once disappointed.

Photographer Sarah Henderson was truly a pleasure to work with, and we couldn't be more pleased with the beautiful images she contributed.

We are thankful for the cheerful participation of the following photo models: Aly Barnheiser, Chuckie Dillard, Rachel Heiber, Stacie Klein, Sam LaTonzea, Elisabeth Limes, Joel Limes, Seamus McCord, Patrick Meehan, and Emmie the cat.

We thank Emily Savors at the Columbus Foundation for always believing in the Next Chapter Book Club. She has been our hero for many years.

We extend our deep appreciation to Larry Fish and Tref Borden at the Fish Family Foundation for their continued support of our mission.

Introduction

After fifteen years of operating book clubs for adults with intellectual and developmental disabilities (IDD), we have had the pleasure of exploring a wide range of reading material for our book club members. From classic children's literature to current young adult fiction, there are indeed a number of excellent books from which our book club members can choose. Yet there remains a noticeable lack of reading material written *specifically for* adults with IDD. Although hi/lo fiction offers reading material for people who do not read at grade level, the majority of hi/lo books target children or teens. The goal of *New Love, Spilt Milk, and Potbellied Pigs*, as well as its prequel, *Lucky Dogs, Lost Hats, and Dating Don'ts*, is to offer adults with IDD stories, plays, and poems that are both relatable and written at an accessible reading level.

Mainly, we wanted to write a book that was fun to read, even for the most challenged adult readers. To accomplish this, the stories, plays, and poems that follow examine universal human emotions and experiences. Most focus on adult themes and include characters with and without disabilities. All pieces in this book are between a second- and fourth-grade reading level (Flesch-Kincaid Grade Level) and are followed by a section called "What Do You Think?" containing both simple and thoughtful discussion questions. We also selected large print, an accessible font style, and photographs to assist with comprehension, all in an effort to appeal to the widest audience possible.

We hope you enjoy your experience with our book!

Warmest wishes,

Tom Fish and Jillian Ober

There's a Cow in the Window

On a warm June day, I turned into the driveway of my aunt and uncle's big old farmhouse. The next day the house would be full of family and friends celebrating the arrival of my first niece, who was expected in August. It was a baby shower. Since I had hosted many baby showers and bridal showers, I was happy to go to my aunt's house a day early to help with all the arrangements.

As I drove down the driveway, I noticed a woman standing at the front door of the farmhouse holding a large pink bathtub. My first thought was, *This person must not know my aunt and uncle. Nobody goes to their front door.* At the farmhouse, everyone goes in and out of the side door. It's just the way it is.

My second thought was, *The pink bathtub must be a gift for the baby shower. But wait! The shower isn't until tomorrow.* I felt bad. This person arrived for the shower a day early.

As I parked my car and got out, the woman walked toward me. Quickly I realized that it was my closest friend from childhood, Anna. She was wearing a lovely yellow dress and carrying another gift in addition to the pink bathtub. I was very happy to see Anna, but I was sad to tell her that she had come to the shower on the wrong day. After a brief hug, we both spoke at the same time.

"The shower isn't until tomorrow," I said.

"There's a cow in the window," Anna said.

"What?" we both asked at the same time.

"The shower isn't until tomorrow," I repeated.

"There's a cow in the window," Anna repeated. She went on to ask, "Did you say the shower is tomorrow?"

"Yes, I'm so sorry," I said. "You must have driven an hour to get here. Gosh, I'm sorry." I watched her facial expression change from confusion to surprise to defeat. She began to cry. I took the big pink bathtub from her hands and set it on the ground. Then I gave her another hug, a longer one, and decided I would ask her about the cow later.

I knew why Anna was crying. A couple months earlier, her brother Jeff found out that he had cancer. It was a very serious and damaging kind of cancer. Jeff was in a lot of pain. Anna and her family were very scared. They had been spending long hours at the hospital with her brother. When she wasn't at the hospital, Anna was worrying about her brother. She also had a full-time job, two young children, and a husband with a broken leg. She was exhausted.

She had been looking forward to the baby shower where she could relax and focus on something positive, if only for a couple hours. When she realized her mistake, she felt overwhelmed with disappointment. She couldn't hold back the tears.

"I'm so sorry. How did I mess this up?" Anna wiped tears from her face, but more tears kept coming. "I can't come back tomorrow because I have to take the kids to a birthday party. Then I need to go see Jeff." Her shoulders dropped. My heart hurt for my friend.

"Well, I'm happy you're here," I said. "We can make our own party! Let's go inside."

"No, I shouldn't. You're getting ready for the shower. I feel so stupid," she said. "How did I mix up Saturday and Sunday?"

"First of all," I said, "you're not stupid. Second, it's no wonder you mixed up the days. You are under way too much stress! You are juggling a full-time job, two young kids, a husband with a broken leg, and everything going on with Jeff. I'm impressed that you made it here at all! You look lovely, by the way."

I picked up the bathtub with one hand and put my other hand on her arm. "Come on, let's go inside, sit down, and have a glass of wine. There's no need for you to turn around and go home right away," I said. We walked through the screened-in porch into the kitchen. My aunt Barb was at the table checking her to-do list.

I told Barb that we had an early guest, and I briefly described the mix-up. Barb laughed warmly, welcomed Anna, and invited her to have a seat. Barb walked over to the cabinet and took out three wine glasses. She pulled the cork on an already-opened bottle and began to pour wine into the glasses.

"But there's still a cow in the window," Anna said.

"I thought that was what you said earlier! What are you talking about? Are you okay?" I asked. I wondered if my friend might be imagining things. After all, I had driven past the house before I pulled into the driveway. *Surely* I would have noticed a cow stuck in a window!

"No, it's in the window well. Let me show you," Anna said.

Barb and I followed Anna outside and around to the front of the house. Beneath each of the large windows on the front of the house were large holes edged with bricks. These holes, or wells, were there to let light from the outside come into the high windows in the basement. There, in the window well just to the left of the front door, was a baby cow.

The calf was curled up inside the window well. Only when we were a few feet away from the well did we spot the stranded calf.

"Oh dear," Barb said.

"Poor thing!" I exclaimed.

"I told you," Anna said. "While I was waiting for someone to answer the front door I noticed the calf move out of the corner of my eye. What should we do?"

At that moment, my cousin Cassie walked around the corner to see what was happening. Barb asked Cassie to go get her father since none of us would be able to lift the lanky calf. It looked like it was well over fifty pounds. "Get your brother, too, please," Barb added.

"It must have come from across the street," I said. Across the street from my aunt and uncle's house was a dairy farm.

My aunt nodded her head. "There must be a gap in the fence somewhere," Barb said. We looked across the street and saw one cow standing very close to the fence, facing us. It seemed to be looking right at us.

"And that must be its mother! Gosh!" said Barb. All of us felt very sorry for the calf and its mother. Soon my uncle Will and cousin Josh came to meet us, and we all stared at the baby cow in the window well.

Will said, "Josh, go tell Jed that we've got one of his calves here. I'm going to go look for something I can wrap around its body to pull it out." After just a few moments, Will returned carrying two long canvas straps.

"Where did you find those?" Barb asked.

"In the shed. I don't even remember what they were for," Will replied. My aunt and uncle had horses on their farm. In addition to a barn, they had a large shed. Both buildings were full of tools and equipment they used on the farm.

"All right now, I'm going to wrap these around the calf and see if I can pull it out," Will said. He squatted down and reached into the window well. The calf seemed frozen.

"It must be scared with all of us staring down at her," I said. "Is there anything we can do to help?"

"Well, no. I just need to lift its front end and reach the strap..." Will stopped talking as the lifting got heavy.

As we were watching Will wrap the straps around the calf, Josh returned from the dairy farm. He was carrying a two-liter soda bottle with a large nipple on the end. It was full of milk.

"Jed said we could use this milk to help the calf calm down and trust us. Plus, we don't know how long it's been in the window! It's probably starving," Josh said.

"So, is Jed the farmer?" Anna asked.

"Yes. He and his brother inherited the farm from their parents. They haven't taken very good care of the place, unfortunately," Barb said. I looked across the street and noticed parts of the main barn that were falling down.

"Poor cows," said Anna.

"Okay!" Will said loudly. "I wrapped the straps around its front end and hind end. Now let's see if I can pull it out."

He was holding the ends of the straps. He bent down and began to pull. The calf began to wiggle. Will was sweating, but he seemed to be enjoying the challenge.

Will pulled harder and the calf began to move. Slowly, Will hoisted the calf up and pulled it onto the grass. It sprang up onto its feet more quickly than any of us expected. It stood still and looked around for a moment, and then sat back down.

"Hooray! Well done, Will!" Shouts and praises came from the small crowd of us watching the action.

"Josh, why don't you see if it wants some milk?" suggested Cassie. Josh picked up the two-liter bottle full of milk. He took a few slow steps toward the calf and put the bottle in front of the calf's nose. It sniffed the bottle. Then it opened its mouth and began to drink the milk. It drank quickly and noisily.

"Oh, get this, everybody! While Jed was filling the bottle for me," Josh began, "he said, 'you know, I noticed the calf's mother standing at the fence most of the day. I wondered why she was just staring across the street at your house.'"

"You're kidding," my aunt Barb said. "She must have seen the calf wander over here. Didn't Jed think it was odd that her calf wasn't with her?"

"I guess not," Josh said.

My aunt and uncle talked about how lovely the dairy farm used to be. They told a funny story about the night the cows got out and wandered onto their lawn.

"There were so many cows outside our window that the mooing woke us up!" Will said. Then he turned his attention back to the task in front of him. "Josh, will you go get the tractor? Pull it right up here, please."

A couple minutes later we heard the sound of the tractor engine. Josh drove the tractor right through the front yard and stopped next to us. Will told him to lower the bucket. Slowly the large, scoop-like part on the front of the tractor lowered down. Will looked at the calf and asked, "Are you ready to go see your mama?"

He bent down and picked up the calf. Now that it wasn't wedged in the window well, the calf was much easier to pick up. He carried it a couple steps and then sat down in the bucket of the tractor with the calf on his lap. To everyone's delight, the calf began to nuzzle my uncle's face. Will smiled a big smile and nuzzled right back.

"Okay, are you ready?" Josh asked. Will gave him a thumbs-up and the tractor started to move slowly back to the driveway. Josh drove carefully across the street and turned into the driveway of the farm.

From across the street, we watched the calf's mother walk slowly along the fence line. She was following the tractor and keeping her eyes on her baby in the front. When the tractor got close to the barn, the mother cow began to run.

"She's running! I don't think I've ever seen a cow run!" Anna exclaimed.

"The mother and child reunion," sang my aunt Barb. This old song by Paul Simon was a perfect fit for the moment. We watched the calf walk into the pasture. Its mother smelled and licked and smelled and licked some more. Mother and child were reunited.

We turned to walk back into the house to drink the wine my aunt had poured earlier. A thought occurred to my cousin Cassie.

"You know, Anna, if you had come tomorrow instead of today, you probably would have seen other people walking in the side door. So, you wouldn't have gone to the front door. Nobody *ever* uses our front door!" Cassie said.

"Oh, I didn't know that," Anna said.

"Well, if you hadn't been knocking on our front door today we would never have known about the calf!" Cassie said.

"You're right, Cassie. The poor cow could have died there!" I said.

"That settles it. You were meant to be here today," said my aunt Barb.

"Well, I guess I don't feel so sad about missing the baby shower tomorrow," Anna said with a smile.

We all agreed that Anna's mix-up was actually a very good thing. Sitting around the kitchen table a few moments later, we raised our wine glasses for a toast.

"To Anna," Barb said. "Saver of baby cows and welcomed guest."

"To Anna!" we all said, and clanked our glasses together.

"Aww, thank you," Anna said. "To mother and baby cow," she said, and we all toasted again.

What Do You Think?

1. In the beginning of the story we learn that Anna is scared and sad because her brother has cancer. What would you do to comfort a friend who is scared and sad?

2. Have you ever had to respond to a crisis? If so, what was it like?

3. Have you ever been to a baby shower? If so, what was it like?

4. What is your favorite kind of farm animal? Some common farm animals are cows, horses, chickens, pigs, sheep, and goats. What if you woke up and your yard was covered with clucking chickens or mooing cows?

A Hug in a Mug

My name is Ethan. On Saturday mornings I like to walk to the library and check out a book. Then I walk to the coffee shop near my apartment building and read the book while I sip my coffee. I also like to read when I get in bed at night. It helps me feel sleepy. I like books with big print and some pictures. Really long books with tiny letters are not as fun for me to read.

The librarians at my library are very kind and smart. They seem to know which books I would like. They make a special pile of books just for me to look at when I come in on Saturday mornings. My favorite librarian, Olivia, reminds me that these books are "just suggestions." The library has so many different books, CDs, and DVDs! Sometimes I like to walk around and look at all the different books in the library. People say I shouldn't pick a book just because of the picture on the cover, but every now and then I do. On other days, I am thankful that Olivia and other librarians have helped me find the kinds of books I usually like.

The coffee shop where I like to read is called The Roast House. They roast coffee beans in the back of the shop and it smells so good in there! There are tables and chairs in The Roast House. There are also comfortable chairs and couches, which I like. The best part of going to The Roast House is seeing my friend Hank. Hank is probably the same age as my grandpa. Hank has dark wrinkled skin and a big smile. Hank likes to sit in the comfy chairs like I do.

One Saturday morning, Hank asked me, "Ethan, do you live near here?"

"Yes," I said. "I live in the apartment building on Birch Avenue. You know the one with the pool?"

"Yes, I know that building. It must be nice to have a pool," Hank said. I nodded my head. I really like to swim when the weather is nice.

"Where do you live?" I asked Hank.

"My house is just a block from here. My wife and I have lived in our house for almost fifty years," Hank said.

"Fifty years? Wow. Haven't you ever wanted to move?" I asked.

Hank sighed. Then he said, "Yes, I have, but my wife is very fond of the house. She doesn't like to leave the house. Our son Cameron moved away for college. I had hoped we might move to be near him, but that didn't happen."

"Why not?" I asked.

"Cameron met a woman from a city called Winnipeg. After they got married, that is where they decided to live. Winnipeg is in Canada, in the province of Manitoba. Do you know where that is?" Hank asked.

"I know where Canada is," I said.

"Manitoba is right in the middle of Canada. It is very cold there in the winter. Too cold for my wife and me. Well anyway, I get up to visit Cam and his family once a year, during the summer. They have four children and busy schedules, so it is difficult for them to travel," Hank explained. Then he sighed and smiled. "I better head home now. As always, it's been a pleasure to see you, Ethan."

"You too, Hank. Maybe your wife will come to The Roast House with you some Saturday? I would like to meet her," I said.

"I wish she could, Ethan. Her health is not good. It is hard for her to walk now. She doesn't like to leave the house. But I've told her about you. She thinks we have a nice friendship," Hank said.

I smiled. I liked it when Hank called me his friend. "What is your wife's name?" I asked.

"Amelia," Hank said, with one hand already on the door.

"Tell Amelia I said 'hi,'" I said.

"Okay, I will," Hank said. Then he opened the door and waved goodbye.

I thought about Hank for the rest of that day. When the next Saturday came, I was excited to see him. At the library, I decided to check out a book about Canada. I thought Hank could show me where his son lived. The book had maps in it. But I didn't see Hank at The Roast House that day.

I was disappointed, but I sipped my coffee and looked at all the colorful maps. I found Manitoba in the middle of Canada, just like Hank had said.

Four more Saturdays went by and Hank did not come to the coffee shop. I missed seeing him and I was starting to worry. Had something happened to him? Hank said he lived a block from the coffee shop, but I didn't know which direction or which house. I decided to ask the people at The Roast House if they knew Hank.

"Sure, we know Hank. He is one of our 'regulars,' like you, Ethan," Kyle, one of the workers, said.

"I haven't seen Hank in a month. Have you?" I asked.

"Now that you mention it, he hasn't been here in a little while. Whenever I see him next I'll tell him you asked about him," Kyle said.

"Okay, thanks," I said.

I was worried. Why hadn't Hank been going to The Roast House? I sat down with my coffee and flipped through the pages of the book I had checked out of the library earlier.

This book was about a lion, a witch, and something called a wardrobe. It had some pictures in it, but it looked a little harder than most of the books I read. I was hoping Hank could help me with it. I started to read the book but I couldn't concentrate. I decided to walk home.

As I was leaving, I saw Hank walking toward The Roast House. I was so pleased! Hank was okay. My worries went away. I walked toward Hank.

"Hank!" I said. "You haven't been here! I'm glad you're okay. I have a new book," I said. I reached into my bag and showed him the book I had checked out of the library that day.

"Oh, that's a dandy, indeed," Hank said. He didn't smile, though. "Ethan, I came here today to tell you that I am going to be moving away, and I may not get to see you again."

I was shocked and sad. "I don't want you to move," I told him.

"I appreciate that." Hank put his hand on my shoulder.

I wanted to hug Hank. He looked sad, too. He also looked very tired.

"What is wrong, Hank?" I asked.

"How about we get a cup of coffee and I will tell you?" Hank suggested.

"I already had my coffee. I shouldn't have more than one cup," I said.

"All right. Well, how about we take a seat on the bench over there," Hank said. I nodded my head and followed Hank across the street to a nearby park bench.

"When I saw you last month, I told you that my wife was not well. Later that week she became very sick. I tried to take her to the doctor, but she wouldn't let me. I think I told you that she doesn't like to leave the house?" Hank asked.

"Yes, I think so," I said.

"A few days went by, and then one morning she fainted. I called nine-one-one. We spent a day in the hospital, and Amelia insisted that we go home. She died at home two days later," Hank said.

Now he looked even more tired than he had when I first saw him.

"I'm sorry," I said. I wanted to make my friend feel better. But I didn't know how. My brother told me that if someone is sad, it is better to listen and not talk. So, that is what I did.

"Amelia had something called multiple sclerosis. People usually call it MS. I don't know what you know about MS, but she lived with it for a long time. It was difficult for her to walk, so she used a scooter to get around at home. We thought she was doing well. We had no idea that Amelia had developed a heart condition. By the time she got sick, it was too late." Hank looked up and stopped talking for a moment.

"Amelia was a stubborn woman. She was stubborn and thoughtful and I loved her. I should have just taken her to the doctor," Hank said. Then he cleared his throat. "Well, anyway, I wanted you to know why you won't see me at The Roast House anymore. I am headed to Canada in three weeks."

"But I thought Canada was too cold for you," I reminded Hank.

"I'm not looking forward to the cold winters. But my son and his family invited me to come and live with them. I think this is the right thing to do. I hardly know my grandchildren," Hank said.

"I'm really going to miss you," I said.

"I'm going to miss you, too. I thought we might exchange addresses. We could be pen pals, if you like. I think people would call that 'old school' now," Hank said. For the first time that morning, I saw a small smile on his face.

"Sure, let me give you my address," I said. I pulled out a notebook and pencil from my library bag. I wrote down my address. I tore out the page and gave it to Hank.

"Thank you, friend. Hand me the notebook, and I'll write down my address for you," Hank said. I handed him the pencil and notebook, and he wrote down his address.

"Will you come to The Roast House before you move? We can still meet there next Saturday, right?" I asked.

"I'm afraid I have too much work to do at home. My son and grandkids will help me with most of the packing and heavy lifting, but there's fifty years' worth of stuff in that house. I have to sort through it all before the moving truck arrives," Hank said.

"Can I help?" I asked.

Hank thought for a moment, and then he said, "That would be nice, Ethan. Thank you. How does next Saturday sound? I have a special project you can help me with."

"Good. I will see you next Saturday. Is ten thirty okay?" I asked.

"That's perfect," Hank said. "I hope you don't mind a little physical labor?"

"No, I don't mind," I replied.

"Great, I will see you next week." Hank stood up and walked away slowly.

I watched him walk. I wondered how old he was. I wondered how sad it would feel to have your wife die. I wondered what our special project was going to be.

***

The next Saturday, I arrived at Hank's house right on time. I knocked on the door. I heard him tell me to "come on in." I turned the doorknob and opened the front door. I saw what fifty years' worth of stuff looked like. There were piles of papers and folders all over the place. Trinkets and other pretty things were on tables, in cabinets, and on shelves. The walls were covered with paintings and photos. Plus, there were tables and lamps and chairs and so much furniture.

"Hello there," I heard Hank say as I walked into the front room from the hallway. "I'm glad you are here. Can I get you anything? A cup of coffee?"

"Yes, please," I said.

I followed Hank into the kitchen. The counters were covered with plates, bowls, and coffee mugs. "Is this the stuff that used to be in your cabinets?" I asked.

"Well, mostly," Hank said. He poured me a cup of coffee and handed it to me. He refilled his coffee and we sat down at the kitchen table. Hank pushed a stack of papers to the side so we could set our mugs on the table.

"I have a card for you," I said. I had bought a sympathy card for Hank the day before. I liked what the card said. I wasn't sure what else to write on the card, so I decided just to write, "Sincerely, your friend Ethan." I hoped the card would make Hank feel better. I pulled it out of my library bag and handed it to him.

Hank took the card, and before he even opened it, he put it between his hands and said, "Thank you, Ethan. I appreciate you thinking about me." Then he opened the card, read it, and put it back in the envelope. "I will take this to Canada with me." We smiled at each other.

I looked around and saw a glass cabinet full of coffee mugs. "You have a lot of things, especially coffee mugs!" I said.

"Yes, everyone knows I like to drink coffee. Over the years people have given me a lot of coffee mugs. I was thinking I would donate my collection to The Roast House. What do you think?" Hank asked. "A lot of people like to drink coffee out of paper cups nowadays, but some of us still like a nice sturdy mug."

"I like mugs. I think The Roast House would like your mugs," I said.

"Why don't you pick out a mug that you would like to keep? I have plenty to go around," Hank said.

"Okay! Thanks, Hank," I said. I walked over to the cabinet and looked at all the mugs. Some were from places like Niagara Falls and San Francisco. Others said things like, "World's Greatest Dad" or "Merry Christmas." Then I saw a mug that said, "Coffee is a hug in a mug" and I picked it up. It was green with white letters. I liked it. "Can I have this one, Hank?" I asked.

"Sure. It's all yours," said Hank. "Are you finished with your coffee? We've got a project to do."

I picked up my coffee and finished it in one big gulp. It was warm and comforting...like a hug in a mug. I set the mug down and Hank said, "All right then, follow me."

Hank got up slowly. I followed him down the hallway to a small room filled with books and papers. "Is this your office?" I asked.

"Yes, this is my office. Amelia called this my 'hiding spot.' I have spent a lot of time in here, reading and writing and thinking," Hank said.

The desk in Hank's office was covered in books and papers. There was also an old leather chair in the corner. It reminded me of the chairs Hank and I liked to sit in at the coffee shop. Next to the chair was a small table with a lamp. The only other things in the room were books. So many books! All the walls had bookshelves, and all the bookshelves were full. There were even stacks of books on the floor.

"I can't take all these books to my son's house. I can't even take *half* of these books. Our mission, if you choose to accept it, is to sort all of these books into piles," Hank said.

"Okay," I said. "What are the piles?"

"Good question," said Hank. "One small pile will be books that I am going to keep or give to my grandchildren. I want to sell some of the nicer books to the used bookstore; those books will go in one pile. Another pile of books will be those I'm going to donate to the library. The last pile will be the books that you would like to have."

I was surprised. I didn't expect Hank to give me any books. "Me? You are going to give me books?" I asked Hank.

"Of course! You and I like books. We like to read. We like to talk about the books we read. And you are my friend. I can't think of anyone else who should have the books, can you?" Hank asked.

"I guess not," I said. I wasn't sure what to say. All I could think to say was "thank you," so that is what I said.

Hank replied, "You are quite welcome."

He was sitting on the small desk chair and he had already started to sort the books on top of his desk into piles.

"How do I know which books go in which piles?" I asked.

"Another good question," Hank said. "Here is what I am thinking. I have a bad shoulder and a not-so-good back. Books can be very heavy, you know. I was hoping you could help me by pulling the books off the shelves. I will take a quick look at them and decide which pile they go in. Then you can put them in the right pile. We will run out of space quickly in here. So, as the piles get larger, I would appreciate you moving them to the bedroom across the hall," Hank said.

I stepped across the hall into the guest bedroom. This room had more empty space than any other room in Hank's house. A moment later, Hank walked into the room with some Post-it notes and a pen. On separate notes he wrote the words, "Keep"; "Sell"; "Donate"; and "Ethan."

"Okay, let's see..." Hank walked slowly around the room and put the Post-it notes on the wall, closet door, and dresser. "Books I am *selling* will go here, books I'm *donating* will go there..."

Hank explained how we would keep track of the books.

I was a little nervous about mixing things up. "I hope I don't get it wrong," I said.

"If you have any questions, all you have to do is ask. I believe you will do just fine. But we will go slowly at first. How does that sound?" Hank said.

"Sounds good," I said. "Let's do this!"

We started on our project. I showed the books to Hank as I pulled them off the shelves. If he didn't want to keep the book, he asked me if I wanted it. Most of the time neither of us wanted the books, so they went into the "Sell" or "Donate" piles. When the piles got big, I moved them to the bedroom across the hall. Hank went with me the first couple of times, but I got the hang of it pretty quickly. We were clearing shelves in no time.

Every now and then, I would show Hank a book and he would clap his hands together and say, "Oh, that one is a dandy." If Hank didn't want to keep the book, I would put it in my pile. Hank kept some of the "dandies" and I kept the rest.

I trusted Hank's opinions about books. I figured, if Hank likes this story, I bet I will, too. I also kept some other books that looked interesting to me.

As we got close to the end of the books, I looked at how many books were in the "Sell" and "Donate" piles. These piles had most of the books. I counted sixteen books in the pile of books I was keeping. Hank's small pile of books stayed next to him, on the floor by his chair.

"The last shelves," I said as I started pulling books from the top shelf of a small bookcase.

We cleared the top shelf. I pulled the first book from the second shelf and recognized the cover. "Hey, this is the book I returned to the library this morning!" It was *The Lion, the Witch and the Wardrobe* by C. S. Lewis.

"That one is a dandy," Hank said with a smile. "How did you like it?" he asked.

"Well, it was kind of hard. I only read the first chapter," I said, feeling bad that I hadn't finished the book.

"That's all right, Ethan. This is a challenging book; you are right about that. I wish I had time to read it with you. That darn moving truck is coming too soon," Hank said. He reached his arm out and said, "Hand me the book, will you?"

I handed the book to Hank. He looked at the cover and rubbed his hand across it. Then he opened the book and sniffed. Hank told me once that he liked the way books smelled. I thought that was funny.

Hank turned to the very beginning of the book. His eyes got wide and he smiled. He was looking at the page that had all the numbers and addresses and dates. I never paid much attention to that page, but Hank was still looking at the page and smiling.

Finally, he said, "We've got a dandy here, for sure. This book is a first edition. Do you know what that means?"

I shook my head.

"That means that *this* book, the one in my hands, was one of the very first copies of *The Lion, the Witch and the Wardrobe* printed in 1950 in London. Goodness, I forgot I had this!" Hank seemed to be very happy about the book. He turned the pages and one of them fell out. Hank carefully put the page back. He looked at the outside of the book. It looked old and dusty and was a yellowish color.

"Well, it's not in very good shape," Hank began, "but it is *still* a first edition. That means it is worth some money."

"Really? How much?" I asked.

"I am not in the collecting business, so I couldn't tell you," Hank said. Then he closed the book and nodded his head, like he had made a decision. He handed the book to me. "I would like you to have it."

"Are you sure? Don't you want to sell it?" I asked.

"No, I would like you to have it. If you decide to read the book, I could talk about it with you over the phone if you like...after I get settled at my son's house," said Hank.

I looked at the book and said, "I will try to read it again. Thank you."

"You don't have to, Ethan. If you decide to sell it, that is up to you. Once you give a gift, you don't get to decide what the person does with it," Hank said. He sat up tall in his chair. "All right then, we are almost finished. Let's go through the last few shelves and then treat ourselves to a cup of coffee. I have decaf for you," Hank said.

Hank remembered that I only drink one cup of coffee per day. Hank was a very nice man. He was generous. I felt sad that his wife had died, and I felt sad that he was moving away.

"I'm going to miss you when you move," I told Hank.

"I will miss you too, Ethan," Hank said.

We finished the last few shelves and moved into the kitchen for coffee. Decaf for me.

Two Months Later

I sat in my favorite comfy chair at The Roast House, drinking coffee out of one of the mugs that Hank donated to the coffee shop. I kept the mug that said "Coffee is a hug in a mug" at home. The one I had in my hand had a picture of a cat on it. It said "Stop Stressing Meowt."

I brought the copy of *The Lion, the Witch and the Wardrobe* that Hank had given me to the coffee shop. A week earlier, I got to see the movie version of *The Lion, the Witch and the Wardrobe*. I really liked it, so I decided to begin reading the book again. I thought, *Now that I know the story, the book won't be so hard to understand*. I was right! I had been reading at home, and now I was on the third chapter.

Before I opened the book to read, I looked up and saw Kyle wiping off tables. He smiled at me.

"Hi, Kyle," I said.

"Hey, man," Kyle said. "What are you reading today?"

"*The Lion, the Witch and the Wardrobe*," I told him. "Hank gave me this book. He said it is a first edition."

Kyle's eyes got wide. "No way," he said. "*First edition?* Can I see it?" Kyle asked. I nodded my head and Kyle walked over to me. I handed him the book, and he went to the front page, the one with all the numbers on it.

"No way! First edition! How cool. Man, I loved *The Chronicles of Narnia*. That's the series of books *The Lion, the Witch and the Wardrobe* is from," Kyle said. He handed the book back to me and said, "That book has to be worth some money. It isn't in great shape, but still, I bet it's worth at least a thousand dollars."

My eyes got wide. "You think this book could be worth a thousand dollars?" I asked Kyle.

"Probably more than that. A friend of mine collects rare books. This isn't the kind of book she would like, but I'm sure she could tell us how much it's worth," Kyle said. "Wait, let's just look it up!"

Kyle pulled out his smart phone and searched the internet. He talked to himself as he typed. "Definitely used book. Condition? I'd say 'fair.'" Then he looked at me and said, "Are you ready?"

I nodded my head again. "You could get four thousand to five thousand dollars for that book. Nice, man! Hank gave you a pretty rad gift," Kyle said. "Okay, I have to get back to work. Enjoy your book!" Kyle went right back to wiping tables.

I tried to go back to reading, but it was no use. I couldn't stop thinking about the first edition book and the money and my friend Hank.

What Do You Think?

1. What should Ethan do with the book? Should he keep it? Sell it? Should Ethan ask Hank if he wants it back?

2. When Hank told Ethan that his wife died, Ethan told Hank that he was sorry. How do you comfort your friends when they share sad news?

3. Hank had to pack up and move to a new city. Have you ever moved to a new city? What was that like?

4. Ethan and Hank were "regulars" at The Roast House coffee shop. That means they were there regularly, or frequently. Are you a "regular" anywhere?

B-Flat Goes Sharp

Cast of Characters:

1. Bonnie

2. Hal

3. Rex

4. Willow

5. Matt

6. Irene

7. Jason

8. Narrator (The narrator tells the readers what the characters are doing. This person reads all *italicized*, or *slanted*, words.)

Act I

<u>Narrator</u>: *This play is about a music store. The name of the store is B-Flat. Hal and Bonnie just bought the store. When they were teachers at the local high school, Hal and Bonnie used to dream about having their own music store. Now they own B-Flat, where Rex, Willow, and Matt give music lessons. Bonnie's mom, Irene, hangs out at B-Flat and gives advice to anyone who will listen. Jason is a high school student who helps tune instruments and clean the store.*

When the play starts, Bonnie and Hal are in B-Flat. Bonnie is putting new things on a shelf, and Hal is sweeping. Bonnie stops for a moment and looks around the store.

<u>Bonnie</u>: Sometimes I wonder if it was a good idea to buy this store, Hal. It needs so much work! The walls need to be painted. We need to soundproof the lesson rooms. We do not have enough students, and we need to sell more instruments.

<u>Hal</u>: Anything else, Bonnie?

Bonnie: Well, the B-Flat sign is so small. How will anyone driving by notice the store?

Hal: I know you are worried, my love. So am I. But we always dreamed of having our own music store, right? Here we are!

Bonnie: I know, Hal. I am excited. But I am also nervous. There is so much that needs to change here. It could be years before we make any money!

Hal: Do you remember what you said to me when I was nervous about buying the store? You told me, "We can do this," and you were right! We have to stay positive.

Narrator: The front door opens and Rex, the drum teacher, walks in.

Rex: What's happening, dudes?

Hal: Hi, Rex. Honestly, right now Bonnie and I are feeling a bit overwhelmed by all the things we need to do to fix up B-Flat.

Rex: Yo, B-Flat is cool. I love the vibe here.

Bonnie: I'm glad, Rex. Maybe you could tell more people about the cool vibe here? We need more music students and customers.

Rex: I can do that.

Hal: Also, how about you show your students the drums and drumsticks for sale?

Rex: You got it, man. I'm on it.

Narrator: *Willow, the guitar teacher, and Matt, the piano teacher, walk out of the rooms where they had been giving lessons.*

Willow: What's going on, guys? You all look concerned.

Bonnie: I suppose we *are* concerned. We haven't had many customers this month, and we have fewer students coming in for lessons. Plus, the store needs a lot of painting and updating. Hal and I have a lot to do and it feels overwhelming right now.

Matt: I hear you. But you guys are not in this alone. Willow and Rex and I love this place. And we have some very loyal customers.

Hal: That's true, Matt.

Willow: My last student said he has been coming to B-Flat since he was a little boy. You know, Hal, Matt and I both teach at the high school, like you and Bonnie used to. We could hang up some flyers on the bulletin boards.

Hal: That would be great, Willow. Thanks, guys.

Narrator: Bonnie's mom, Irene, comes out of the bathroom.

Irene: We are going to need more toilet paper, Bonnie. What kind of place are you running here?

Bonnie: Not now, Mom.

Irene: What? What's wrong?

Bonnie: Hal and I are feeling overwhelmed. Running a music store is not easy, especially when we do not have enough customers and students.

Irene: Is there anything I can do to help?

Bonnie: Well, you could tell your friends to send their grandchildren for music lessons.

Matt: Irene, don't you go to the senior center?

Irene: Yes, every Tuesday and Friday.

Matt: They have a piano there, right?

Irene: Yes, but nobody ever plays it.

Matt: I could go there once a week and give piano lessons. We are never too old to learn new things.

Irene: That's the truth. I will ask around the next time I am there. Willow, I heard you say something about flyers?

Willow: Yes, I was going to make some to hang up at school.

Irene: Print me a stack, will you? I go lots of places. I will put them all over town.

Willow: Sure thing!

Narrator: Irene turns to Bonnie and Hal.

Irene: You need to do more advertising and replace that small sign. No one can see it from the road.

Bonnie: Yes, we know, Mom. Hal and I want to get some work done in the store before we spend money on advertising.

Irene: Well, you can put an ad in the newspaper for free, I think.

Hal: We started doing that last week. But the ad is so small, just like our sign. I wonder if anyone notices it.

Irene: Okay, well then, we should start with the walls in here. A fresh coat of white paint would brighten up the space.

Bonnie: I was actually thinking about painting the inside of the store a soothing ivory color.

Willow: Oh, ivory would be so much nicer than this swampy green color!

Matt: We can all help paint.

Willow: Do you see, Bonnie and Hal? We are a team.

Bonnie: You guys are awesome. Thank you. Hal and I will take all the help we can get!

Narrator: Everyone gets back to work. The mood is happier now. Rex turns the music up in the store and sings along with "Born in the USA" by Bruce Springsteen.

Act II

Narrator: A couple days later, Willow and Matt are alone in the teachers' room at the high school.

Willow: I hope we can help Bonnie and Hal.

Matt: Me too. Just think about it; they were teachers like us, and now they own their own music store. They are living their dream!

Willow: Except it seems like more of a nightmare for them right now. It must be stressful to run a store. I am glad they're going to the winery this weekend for their anniversary. They need some time to relax.

Matt: Are you thinking what I'm thinking?

Willow: Matt! We can't kiss here at school!

Matt: I know. But I can do this...

Narrator: Matt blows Willow a kiss. Willow catches it and smiles.

Matt: I was actually thinking about painting the store while Bonnie and Hal are away this weekend.

Willow: I like this idea! It can be an anniversary surprise for Bonnie and Hal. I will talk to Jason after math class. I think he is supposed to work at the store this weekend.

Matt: Great! I will talk to Rex and Irene.

Narrator: Matt blows Willow another kiss.

Willow: I wonder...

Matt: What do you wonder?

Willow: I wonder if anyone knows about *us*.

Matt: I doubt it. How would anyone know? We do not act like boyfriend and girlfriend in front of anybody.

Willow: I know, but I am tired of keeping our relationship a secret.

Matt: I thought we wanted to make sure our relationship did not get in the way of doing a good job at school and at the store. Remember, you told me that sometimes work and romance do not mix well.

Willow: Yes, I remember. That was four months ago. Have we had any problems here at school or at B-Flat?

Matt: Nope.

Willow: Well, then I think we can be open about it now. I do not like keeping secrets.

Matt: Okay, I'm with you! We should tell the principal first. Then, no more secrets...except for one.

Willow: What are you talking about?

Matt: Our plans for B-Flat this weekend!

Willow: Oh, right!

Narrator: The bell rings and Matt and Willow head off to their classrooms. Later that afternoon, Willow asks Jason if he can stay for a couple minutes after math class to talk. Jason agrees.

Willow: How do you like your job at B-Flat, Jason?

Jason: I like it. I do not like to clean the store as much as I like to tune the guitars and other instruments. Everyone is nice there. My parents say B-Flat is a good place for me to work.

Willow: I agree. You have an amazing ability to know when an instrument is out of tune. I like working at B-Flat, too.

Jason: Also, your boyfriend works there.

Willow: Yes, he does. How did you know that Matt is my boyfriend?

Jason: The kids at my lunch table were talking about it. Were they wrong?

Willow: No, they were not wrong. But we tried to keep it a secret. I wonder how anyone found out.

Jason: They said he smiles at you a lot.

Narrator: Willow smiles when she hears Jason say that.

Jason: They also said you smile at him a lot, too.

Willow: I guess we do smile at each other a lot! But that is not what I wanted to talk to you about. I wanted to ask you if you would like to help us surprise Hal and Bonnie this weekend.

Jason: Okay. What is the surprise?

Willow: Hal and Bonnie need some help at the store. They are going out of town for their anniversary this weekend. Matt and I thought we could all meet at B-Flat to paint and do some other projects. Would you like to join us?

<u>Jason</u>: Sure! Count me in.

Act III

<u>Narrator</u>: Rex, Jason, and Irene are at B-Flat early Friday evening. Everything has been moved into the center of the space. Rex and Jason are wearing old clothes and getting ready to start painting. Irene is putting sheets and blankets over all the instruments and supplies so no paint will get on them.

<u>Rex</u>: Hey, Jason, can you help push this piano away from the wall? I think we should be ready to start the painting party after that.

<u>Narrator</u>: Jason and Rex push the heavy piano a few feet away from the wall. Irene pulls a big sheet over the piano.

<u>Irene</u>: It is a good thing you had those old painting tarps, Rex. We've got every sheet, tablecloth, and blanket I own draped over the instruments!

Rex: Yeah, you should see my garage. I never throw anything away. You name it, I got it. Including giant plastic tarps!

Irene: I guess we're just waiting on Willow and Matt to get here with the paint and supplies. Jason, it was so kind of your parents to pay for all of that! Please be sure to thank them for us.

Jason: I will. My mom likes to decorate. She was excited to go to the paint store and pick out the color.

Irene: I'm glad Willow and Matt both went to pick up the paint. They have six gallons of paint to carry!

Rex: Shoot, Matt wouldn't miss a chance to be alone with Willow.

Irene: What do you mean?

Rex: They're sweet on each other. Can't you tell?

Irene: Really? Well, now that you mention it, they do come in and out of the store together a lot. Jason, do you know about this?

Jason: Yes. People at school were talking about it.

Irene: Really?

Narrator: Just then, Willow and Matt walk in the door of B-Flat. They are carrying paint and supplies. Jason and Rex go to Willow's car to help carry in the rest of the paint. When everyone is inside the store, Irene looks at Matt and Willow.

Irene: It is nice of the two of you to finally show up. You are late, you know. What have you been up to?

Matt: I'm sorry we are late. The paint store only had one gallon of paint ready! We had to wait for them to mix the other five gallons.

Willow: It took forever!

Irene: Or maybe you two lovebirds got distracted, staring into each other's eyes...

Narrator: Irene laughs. Willow and Matt look at each other and then at Irene.

Matt: Lovebirds? I don't see any lovebirds here.

Narrator: Willow walks over to Matt and puts her arm around him.

Willow: I think they figured it out, honey.

Irene: Rex and Jason knew, but I just found out! You make a very cute couple, by the way. Oh, I can't wait to tell Bonnie!

Rex: All right, brothers and sisters, let's get to work. We have a lot to do and only a weekend to do it. Willow, how about you and I start painting the edges and corners? Matt, Irene, and Jason, you can use the rollers to paint the walls.

Willow: Sounds like a plan. Jason, I know it is uncomfortable for you to get things on your hands. Have you thought about wearing the gloves you usually wear when you clean?

Jason: I already have them.

Narrator: Jason pulls out a pair of rubber gloves from the pocket of the apron he is wearing. Willow gives Jason a thumbs-up.

Rex: This place is going to look groovy when we are done painting.

Matt: Yep, it is going to look sharp!

Irene: That's it! What a great idea! I need to go make a phone call. I will be right back.

Matt: Do you know what Irene is talking about?

Rex, Jason and Willow *at the same time*: Nope.

Narrator: Everyone works hard for the rest of Friday night and Saturday. Irene helps the few customers who come into the store during the day Saturday. After the store closes, the team finishes painting. They also wipe down the shelves, clean the windows and doors, and sweep the floors. On Sunday morning, everyone meets at B-Flat to put the display cases, shelves, and instruments back where they belong. This time, Irene is late to arrive.

Willow: I am exhausted. How about you guys?

Jason: I feel better this morning. I have more energy in the mornings.

Rex: Not me, my man. I am not a morning person. Thank goodness for black coffee.

Narrator: Rex raises his cup of coffee, and Willow raises hers to make a toast to coffee.

Rex: I'll tell you what though, I've never seen this place look so slick.

Matt: I know. Jason, I think your mom picked the perfect shade of ivory.

Narrator: Irene walks in the front door of the store.

Irene: Would one of you help me carry something from my car?

Willow: Sure, what do you have, Irene?

Irene: Oh, just the icing on the cake.

Narrator: Irene gives everyone a wink. Willow follows her outside. A few moments later, the two walk back inside carrying a large sign. Rex helps Irene take the plastic cover off the sign. Then he reads the sign.

Rex: "B-Flat Goes Sharp." Far out, Irene!

Willow: I love it!

Narrator: Jason scratches his head.

Jason: Oh, now I understand. Musical notes can be flat or sharp. But "sharp" can also mean pretty and polished. We painted and cleaned B-Flat, so now it's "sharp." Is that right?

Irene: You got it!

Jason: So there is no icing or cake?

Irene: I'm sorry, no cake. But I almost forgot! I got donuts. They are on the back seat in my car if anyone wants to go get them.

Rex: I'm on it, sister. I need some sugar!

Narrator: Rex goes and gets the donuts from Irene's car. Everyone sits for a minute to enjoy a donut.

Matt: That sign is just so clever, Irene.

Irene: You are the one who gave me the idea, Matt. You said the store would look sharp when we were done. Anyway, the main B-Flat sign is so small. I thought this would be a fun way to attract more customers until Bonnie and Hal can order a bigger B-Flat sign.

Willow: Have you heard from Bonnie or Hal this weekend? Do you know when they will be back in town?

Irene: Yes, they should be back around noon, and I'm sure they will come straight to the store. This is the longest they have been away from B-Flat since they bought the place.

Matt: That gives us about two hours to finish up here.

Narrator: The team gets back to work after they finish their donuts. Willow and Rex hang the sign in the front window. Matt and Jason push cases and shelves back to where they belong. Irene straightens all the things for sale and wipes down the cash register. It is noon, and B-Flat looks very sharp.

Irene: Bonnie just called. She and Hal are just around the corner. She sounded nice and relaxed.

Matt: Good! I think I would be relaxed after a weekend at a winery, too.

Willow: We should go sometime, Matt.

Matt: You got it, babe.

Narrator: Irene notices Hal's car pull into the parking lot.

Irene: They're here!

Narrator: Bonnie and Hal begin to walk into the store, and then stop when they notice the new sign. After they walk through the front door, they stop and look around. Both of them look confused and amazed.

Jason: Is anyone going to yell surprise?

Matt: How about you, Jason?

Jason: Surprise!

Hal: Look at this place! I can hardly believe my eyes!

Bonnie: Who..? How...? When...? Did you all do this?

Irene: You have some wonderful friends here, Bonnie. They volunteered their time and worked hard all weekend. Jason's parents bought all the supplies. The sign is an anniversary gift from me.

Narrator: Bonnie and Hal turn in circles, looking around the store.

Jason: Are you surprised?

Hal: Oh, I'm definitely surprised. I'm also thrilled and inspired and very, very grateful!

Bonnie: I'm completely overwhelmed...but in a good way! Thank you so much! This is just the color I had in mind. Hal, I think *now* would be a good time to enjoy the souvenir we bought at the winery.

Hal: Good idea, Bonnie!

Narrator: Hal reaches into his overnight bag and pulls out a bottle of sparkling wine.

Hal: This is from the winery where Bonnie and I stayed this weekend. We thought we would open it when we had something to celebrate. What better time to celebrate than now?!

Rex: Right on, man. I'll take some bubbly!

Narrator: Hal pops the cork out of the bottle and everyone cheers. Bonnie gets paper coffee cups stacked next to the coffee pot and hands them to everyone except Jason.

Bonnie: I'm sorry, Jason. This has alcohol in it, and you are too young to drink.

Jason: It's okay. I tried wine once with my dad. I would rather have water.

Narrator: *Jason grabs his water bottle and Hal walks around and pours a little sparkling wine into each person's paper cup.*

Hal: I guess this isn't fancy...

Matt: But it is sharp!

Narrator: *Matt points to the new sign and everyone laughs.*

Bonnie: As you know, Hal and I were feeling very overwhelmed before we went away this weekend. We had a wonderful, relaxing weekend together. It helped us to remember what new love felt like. Matt and Willow, you know what I'm talking about.

Willow: Wait! You know, too?! We thought no one knew.

Hal: Oh, you can't hide new love that easily!

Narrator: Matt and Willow blush and smile at each other. Bonnie raises her cup for a toast. The others raise their drinks.

Hal: To B-Flat and the most generous friends anyone could ask for.

<u>Bonnie</u>: Cheers, everyone! And thank you from the bottom of our hearts.

<u>Full cast</u>: Cheers!

What Do You Think?

1. B-Flat is a store that sells musical instruments and equipment. If you could own any kind of store, what kind of store would you have?

2. Why did Matt and Willow want to keep their relationship private? What are other reasons people might decide to keep a relationship private?

3. Have you ever wanted to learn to play a musical instrument? If so, which one?

4. The employees of B-Flat give Hal and Bonnie a very nice surprise. Have you ever been to a surprise party? What was it like?

Yummy As Can Be

I am a chocolate cake,
Ready to be ate.
When people look at me,
Mostly frosting is what they see.

My maker is a baker.
Her name is Betty Lou.
She poured her heart and soul into me,
Then had to sell me at the bakery.

Yummy As Can Be

The bakery's name is Dream Delights.
It gets very busy on Friday nights.
That's when a man came in,
Looking for some chocolate sin

He asked lots of questions of Betty Lou,
Like, "Does your cake have lots of chocolate goo?"
He wanted me for his son's birthday.
Betty Lou got me ready to send away.

The young man got his money ready.
I would be a special treat for his son, Freddy.
He thought how happy his son would be,
When he got me home from the bakery.

Then Betty Lou had a second thought,
She wasn't sure she wanted me bought.
It was hard for her to say,
But she did not want to sell me away.

I meant too much to Betty Lou,
All my frosting and inner goo.
Also today was a special one,
The birthday of her only son...

"I'm so sorry," Betty Lou said.
"How about a red velvet cake instead?"
The young man's eyes lit up.
He got happy as a pup.

"That's perfect," he said.
"My son's favorite color is red!
"Can you write 'Happy Birthday' on top,
"And do it in big letters using chocolate?"

"Sure thing," said Betty Lou.
"Absolutely, can do."
"I am so glad things worked out."
"That way, neither of us has to pout."
"Your son will be happy, and so will mine."
"Things have worked out just fine."

Yummy As Can Be

"A cake for you and a cake for me."
"Now it's time for birthdays that are happy."

Everyone ended up happy,
And that was fine with me.
Because as a chocolate cake,
I always knew my destiny...

Yum, yum, yum!

What Do You Think?

1. If you could have any kind of cake for your birthday, what kind would it be?

2. Have you ever baked a cake? Was it easy or hard to do?

A Walk with Randy

I like to walk. Everyone tells me it is a good thing to do. My mom, dad, and doctor think it is great. They say that walking is good for my health. I am glad about that, but I walk because I really enjoy it. I like to think while I walk. For some reason, it is easier for me to think if my feet are moving. I have heard some people say it is easier for them to think when they are in the bathroom. I think that is funny.

My brother Randy does not care about walking at all. He spends most of his days on the computer. Randy is twenty-three and has autism. I often ask him to walk with me, but he always says no. He would rather be on the computer than go for a walk with his little brother. That is okay with me, though. Like I said, I like to think while I walk.

My name is Ben. I am eighteen years old, and I will graduate from high school in the spring. I live with my brother Randy and my mom and dad. We also have a ten-year-old collie named Shrug. I guess you could say he is part of our family. We live outside Boise, Idaho on a 400-acre potato farm. My dad spends most of his time on the farm. My mom is a second-grade teacher.

You already know I like to walk. I also like music. I play drums in my high school marching band. After graduation, I plan to attend college at the University of Idaho in Moscow, Idaho. I want to study music education. My dream job is to direct a marching band.

This is an exciting time for me. It is also a confusing time. Going to college over five hours away from home sounds exciting, but I wonder if it is the right choice for me. I have never really been away from home before. Running a farm takes a lot of time and attention, so my family never traveled very far. Another reason we did not travel is because Randy is uncomfortable in the car and most other places away from home.

Instead of moving away after I graduate, I could stay home. My dad could always use more help with the farm. My mom could always use help with Randy. Lately, the more I think about moving away from my family, the more unsure I feel.

Last Saturday afternoon I opened a piece of mail from the University of Idaho. It was a brochure about living on campus. I did not know any of the happy, smiling college students on the brochure. I wondered what it would be like to move to a place where I did not know anyone. I felt confused and a little nervous. I needed to think. So, like I usually do when I need to think, I decided to go for a walk.

As I was leaving the house, I yelled out, "Going for a walk! Anyone want to come?"

Most of the time, no one wants to walk with me. On this day, I was counting on it. I wanted to walk alone because I wanted to think.

Someone touched my shoulder from behind. It was Randy.

"I'll go," he said.

"You will?" I asked.

I was surprised. Usually, Randy does not want to go anywhere. He definitely does not like to exercise. But Randy nodded his head.

"All right, brother. Are you sure?" I asked. Randy nodded his head again.

Randy was standing next to the front door in a black shirt, blue jeans, beat-up cowboy boots, and a black cowboy hat. That was pretty much Randy's outfit most of the time.

I wondered about the timing of things. Just when I really needed time alone to think, my brother decided to spend time with me. Then I wondered why Randy wanted to go for a walk all of a sudden.

As we walked outside and got into my truck, I asked Randy, "It's hot out here, Rand. You sure you feel like going for a walk?" Rand is the name I call him.

"Yep," Randy answered. He buckled his seatbelt and looked out the window.

"All right then," I said, and started the truck. Randy cleared his throat and took a deep breath. I know my brother pretty well. I could tell something was bothering him. "What's up, Rand?" I asked.

He mumbled something that sounded like, "Nothing." Then he kept talking. "Well, I don't know. You know my friend Patrick?"

"Yeah, he's the guy you play online games with, right?" I asked. I felt a little bit excited. Randy doesn't usually share much, but this time he had something he wanted to tell me.

"Yeah," Randy answered.

As we drove around a curve in our long driveway, we saw my dad standing near the fence. He took his hat off and waved at us. I thought it would be rude to keep driving, but I didn't want Randy to stop talking.

"Hang on, man. I really want to hear what you have to say. Let's just stop quickly and tell Dad where we're going," I said.

Dad walked toward us with a big smile. I rolled down the window and said, "Hey, old man."

He put one foot up on a fence rail and wiped his sweaty forehead with his sleeve. "Where are you boys headed?" he asked.

"On a walk," answered Randy.

"Oh, yeah? You going to Hyatt Lakes?" Dad asked.

"Probably, if that's okay with Randy?" I looked at Randy and he shrugged his shoulders like he didn't care where we went.

I love going to Hyatt Lakes. It is beautiful there. The website says, "Hyatt Hidden Lakes Reserve is a forty-four-acre haven for birds, animals and people."

Walking can sometimes be boring. But not at Hyatt Lakes. There are lots of different trails and beautiful little lakes. Plus, I always feel better after walking than I did before.

"Hmm," Dad said and scratched his stubbly chin. "That sounds nice. Mind if I tag along?" he asked.

Why did everyone want to go for a walk with me all of a sudden? But before I could answer, Randy looked at Dad and said, "We just want to have some brother time together."

Dad and I were both shocked, but we tried not to show Randy. Instead, I looked at Dad and said, "That's right, brother time. Do you mind?"

"No, no, of course not," Dad answered. "Okay, you guys have a good time." He had a confused look on his face. I could tell he was wondering what was going on with Randy. I looked at my dad and made a facial expression as if to say, "I do not know what this is about either." Dad nodded and smiled.

As we started to drive away, Dad shouted, "Try not to get into too much trouble!"

Then Dad waved and we drove off down the long driveway that led in and out of the farm. The name of our farm is "Two Little Spuds." Mom and Dad named it after Randy and me when we were little kids.

You have to drive around a lot of potholes in our driveway, and it is very dusty, I thought. *I do not know why Dad has not fixed the driveway. Maybe he has too many other things to do. Or maybe he is cheap. I will have to ask him sometime. Dad and I are friends but he does not share much with me. Maybe I do not share enough with him.*

I started to think about my dad and my relationship with him when I remembered that Randy had something to share.

"So, Rand, what were you going to say about Patrick?" I asked.

"He has a girlfriend now. He does not play video games when he is spending time with his girlfriend. I want a girlfriend, too," Randy said.

Randy went on to talk about how hard it was to meet girls. He also talked about being lonely.

I was really glad Randy was sharing his feelings with me. Randy has always had trouble with that. He gets nervous and does not know what to say. I have the same problem sometimes.

"Thank you for telling me this, Rand. I am sorry that you feel lonely. You are right, it *is* hard to meet girls!" I agreed with Randy.

"But at least you have had girlfriends before," Randy said.

He must think I know something about dating, I thought. *Ha!*

"Yes, I did. But remember, I was in the same class at school with those girls. Now that you and I are out of school, it is even harder to meet people. So, we will have to help each other out," I said. I wanted Randy to know that I was always going to be there to help him. "Do you know how Patrick met his girlfriend?"

"On a dating website. I tried it for three months," Randy said.

I had no idea Randy had tried online dating! I had not tried it yet.

89

"Really, you did? Well, what happened?" I asked.

"Nothing happened. I emailed four girls. Only one emailed me back. She wanted to meet for dinner. I can't drive, so..." Randy must not have wanted to ask for a ride. He had tried driving many times, but it made him nervous.

"I understand," I said. I wanted to encourage Randy. "How about—" I wanted to talk about where he might go to meet people, but Randy's phone beeped. He plays a lot of games on his phone. The beep meant it was his turn to play. I knew this meant he would not be talking for a little while.

As we drove toward Boise, there were a lot of mountains to see. There was no snow yet, but there would be plenty of the white stuff in late fall. We also drove by other potato farms. Idaho grows more potatoes than any other state in the US. Idaho potatoes are the best because of all the water that runs off the mountains. We also have very good soil.

Just as we got to the parking lot at Hyatt Lakes, Randy asked, "Are you still going to college in the fall?"

"That's a good question, Rand. I'm thinking about it. There are good reasons to go and good reasons to stay home. It is a tough decision," I said.

"I will miss you if you go," Randy said.

"I will miss you, too. I haven't decided yet though," I said. The thought of Randy missing me made me feel sad.

We got out of the car and did some stretching exercises before the walk. Randy was not sure what to do, so I showed him. His cowboy hat fell off a few times. But he wanted to keep wearing it.

As we walked toward the trail, I saw an ice cream truck. I knew Randy would not miss a chance for ice cream. He walked over to the truck and I followed him. There was an older man and a girl about Randy's age in the truck. Randy started talking to the girl!

How did he have the courage to talk to a woman he had never met before? This was not like Randy. But I did not want to interrupt them. I bought a bottle of water from the man in the truck, walked to a nearby fence and kept stretching.

A couple minutes later, Randy walked toward me with a smile on his face. "That's Autumn. We went to high school together. She lives with her mom and dad, too."

"That's nice," I said. "She's cute, too. Are you going to buy some ice cream?"

"Yes, they have rocket pops. I think I would like to keep talking to Autumn instead of going on a walk. Her dad said she could go on a break now. Do you mind?" Randy asked.

"Of course not, brother. I will meet you back here in forty-five minutes, okay?"

Randy nodded and headed back toward the ice cream truck. I was surprised at how well this was working out. Randy was talking to a girl, and I had time to walk and think.

As I walked, I thought about the brochure from the University of Idaho. Everyone looked so happy in the pictures. I wondered if I would be that happy at college. It could be hard to make new friends. On the other hand, I liked meeting new people. Between my classes and all the clubs and activities on campus, I had a feeling I would really like it there.

I was still unsure about leaving my family and being so far away. *Five hours is a long time to be in a car*, I thought. *It is a really long time for Randy to be in a car.* I doubted that he would ever visit me. That meant I would not see my family very often.

I felt sad about that. Randy had just shared his feelings about wanting a girlfriend. He said he would miss me if I went to college. How could I leave now?

I was coming close to the end of the trail and the ice cream truck where I left Randy. But I still hadn't made up my mind about going to college. I figured I would need to go on a couple more walks before I could make this decision. On the last part of the trail, I just looked around and enjoyed the beauty of nature. I spotted some pretty flowers near the trail and picked them for my mom.

When I got back to the ice cream truck, Autumn was back at work. I looked toward my truck and saw Randy sitting inside with the windows rolled down. He was playing on his phone. I walked over to him.

"Hey, Rand. How was your chat with Autumn?" I asked.

"Fine. I want to take her to the mall. Can you take us sometime?" Randy asked.

"Sure. When do you want to go?" I said. I could hardly believe this was my brother Randy talking.

"Can you take us tomorrow?" he said, still not looking up from his phone.

"Okay, I can take you in the afternoon. Do you want to go ask her while we are here?" I suggested.

"Okay," Randy said. He looked up from his phone and saw the flowers I had in my hand. Then I had an idea.

"I picked these for Mom, but maybe you could give them to Autumn instead?" I had hardly finished talking before Randy opened the door and grabbed the flowers.

A couple minutes later, Randy returned to the truck. He got in, but did not say anything. I got nervous. Maybe Autumn had said no.

"Well, what did she say?" I asked.

"She said yes. She can go at three o'clock. Here is her address," Randy said, and showed me a recent text on his phone with Autumn's address. Then Randy's phone beeped. It was another text. Randy smiled. "She says she likes the flowers."

"Well done, Rand!" I exclaimed.

I had not been able to make a decision about going to college, but Randy had a date! This was a great day.

Mom and Dad were on the porch when we got home. When Randy told them about his date with Autumn, Dad stood up and shook his hand. Mom declared that we would have to celebrate that night with Randy's favorite dessert, brownie sundaes.

***

The next day, Randy dressed in his usual all-black outfit. We left early to make sure we would arrive at Autumn's house on time. On the way, Randy watched the GPS on his phone. "How are you doing, Rand?" I asked. I thought he might be nervous. This was his first date, after all.

"I'm okay," he said. "In five hundred feet, turn right," Randy repeated the GPS directions.

Within a couple of minutes we arrived at Autumn's house. Randy got out of the truck and walked quickly to the front door. After he knocked on the door, Randy stood as still as a statue. He was definitely nervous. I thought back to my first date and remembered how nervous I was.

"You got this, Rand. You got this," I said to myself.

Autumn opened the door and invited Randy inside. A few moments later, Randy, Autumn, and Autumn's parents came outside. I got out of the truck and introduced myself. "Hello, I'm Randy's brother Ben," I said.

"It's nice to meet you, Ben," Autumn's mother said. I shook her hand and then Autumn's father's hand. "We asked Autumn to be home by five thirty. Is that okay with you two gentlemen?" she asked.

"Sure," I said, and looked at Randy. "You got that, Rand? Five thirty?"

"Yes, that's fine," Randy said. He seemed slightly less nervous now, though I could tell he was ready for us to be on our way.

"Bye, Mom. Bye, Dad," Autumn said and waved goodbye to her parents. We piled in the truck, fastened our seatbelts, and headed off to the mall.

"Those are cool orange sneakers, Autumn," I said. Autumn was wearing jean shorts, a blue and white striped top, and flashy orange sneakers. She looked bright and happy, though she did seem a bit shy. Maybe she was nervous, too.

"Thank you," she replied. I hoped that Randy would join the conversation, but he was already looking at his phone. Autumn looked at Randy's phone and noticed the game he was playing. "I play that game, too," she said to Randy. The two began to talk about the different games they played. I was happy they had something in common.

When we got to the mall, we agreed that I would meet them in front of the Apple store at 4:45. Randy loved that store, and apparently, so did Autumn. Feeling glad about the smooth start to Randy's date, I walked to the bookstore to get a cup of coffee and read some magazines. I had been there about twenty minutes when I heard someone say my name.

"Ben, is that you?" the voice said. I looked up to see a friend who had graduated from high school one year before me. His name was Nate. He had been in college throughout the past year. I wondered if he might be able to help me with my own college dilemma.

"Hey, man! Good to see you!" I said. "Are you home for spring break?"

"Yeah, I'm home for the week, hanging out with my family. I can't wait to get back to school though!" Nate said.

"Cool," I said. "Where did you end up going?"

"University of Idaho," said Nate.

"Really? That is where I might go!" I said. "How do you like it there?"

"I don't like it...I love it! There are girls everywhere!" Nate said with a big smile.

"All right, that sounds great," I said, and smiled back at Nate. "But what is it really like? I am just not sure I want to move so far away."

Nate looked shocked. "What? Oh man, you will love it. I guess it is far from home, but you will get used to it. University of Idaho is not too big, not too small. The campus is beautiful and there is so much to do." Nate and I went on to talk about college life. The more we talked, the more excited I felt about going to college.

I looked at my watch. It was almost 5:00. I was late to meet Randy and Autumn.

"Oh, shoot! I was supposed to meet my brother and his date fifteen minutes ago!" I exclaimed.

"Hey, how is Randy?" Nate asked.

"He's good, I think. He's not going to like that I'm late, though," I said. I grabbed my empty coffee cup and napkin and threw them away.

"Cool, man. Tell him I said hi. I will see *you* in Moscow in the fall," Nate said with confidence.

"Well, I am definitely leaning in that direction! Thanks for the chat, man. This was a big help!"

I said goodbye to Nate and raced to the Apple store.

When I got to the store, I did not see Randy or Autumn at first. I started to get nervous. I called Randy on his cell phone and heard his ringtone coming from somewhere in the store. I found him sitting on the floor in the far corner of the store. Autumn was sitting beside him. This was not a good sign.

I walked slowly over to Randy and Autumn. "Hey, Rand. What's going on?" I asked as calmly as I could.

Randy did not answer me. I could see that he was really upset. I looked at Autumn. She sat facing Randy. "Autumn, is everything okay?" I asked.

"Randy was looking at one of the tablets. The store got really crowded and really loud. Then Randy got upset when one of the workers asked us if we needed help. She did not hear him answer the first time, so she asked twice. He shouted 'No!' and then someone bumped into him. They said 'excuse me,' but Randy walked away and sat down here," Autumn explained.

"Oh, gosh. I'm sorry, you guys. How long have you been sitting here?" I asked.

"Twenty minutes," Autumn answered. "I get overwhelmed sometimes, too. I have autism like Randy. I have to take breaks. It is okay to take breaks."

"You are right. Thank you for your help, Autumn," I said. I was so thankful that Autumn was there with Randy. This had happened before. My brother can get upset if there are too many people or too much noise. When I was younger, I would get embarrassed because people would look at us. I do not care about that now. Apparently, Autumn did not care either. She understood.

"We should get going. Rand, are you ready to leave now?" Randy nodded his head.

Randy and Autumn stood up.

Autumn quickly touched Randy on the shoulder.

"Randy, it will be okay," she reassured him.

"Thanks," Randy said quietly.

We walked quickly and quietly to the truck. No one talked on the way home.

As we pulled into Autumn's driveway, Randy said, "Sorry."

"No worries, brother," I said.

"This happens sometimes. It is okay," Autumn said. Then she changed the subject. "Will you be coming back to Hyatt Lakes for another walk? I will be working in the ice cream truck both days this weekend."

"Sure. I think so. Ben, can we go for another walk?" Randy asked.

"You bet. But will you actually *walk* with me this time?" I asked and winked at him. Randy shrugged his shoulders. "I think he would rather talk to you, Autumn," I said.

Autumn smiled. She opened the truck door and I quietly reminded Randy that he should walk his date to her front door. As Randy walked back to the truck, I noticed a smile on his face. He was okay. My brother would be okay without me, and I would go to college.

What Do You Think?

1. How would you finish the story?

2. Do you enjoy taking walks?

3. Do you have a brother or sister? If so, how do you get along?

4. Is it easy or hard to date?

5. What do you know about autism?

Boomtown Bulldogs

Cast of Characters:

1. Calvin Peoples

2. Announcer

3. Coach Bill

4. Rachel

5. Jack

6. Stephanie

7. Mrs. Peoples

8. Mr. Peoples

9. Narrator (The narrator tells the readers what the characters are doing. This person reads all *italicized*, or *slanted*, words.)

Act I

Narrator: This is a play, which is a story that can be acted out on stage. This play is about a basketball game. One player, Calvin Peoples, is having a tough time.

Announcer: Four seconds left on the clock. She decides to take the shot... Oh! So close! Okay, everyone, that's the halftime buzzer. The Boomtown Bulldogs trail the Watertown Wildcats by eighteen points.

Narrator: The crowd cheers and claps for both teams.

Mr. Peoples: Great effort, Bulldogs!

Mrs. Peoples: Way to play, Calvin!

Narrator: The team and Coach Bill walk quietly into the school's locker room.

Calvin: This sucks. This team sucks! My old basketball team never let another team beat us by eighteen points.

Rachel: We're trying, Calvin. The Wildcats are tough.

Coach Bill: You're right, Rachel, the Wildcats are tough. But the Bulldogs are tough too. Give us a chance, Calvin. This is only your second game with us. Now let's talk about some of the things we can do in the second half of the game to score more points.

Calvin: How about asking the other team to leave the court?

Jack [laughing]: Good one!

Coach Bill: Well, I suppose that would work. But I don't think it's an option. What about some other ideas?

Rachel: We need to catch each other's passes. They keep stealing the ball from us.

Jack: I know! I passed Stephanie the ball and it went right over her head. That other girl grabbed the ball, ran down the court, and *swoosh*! She made a basket.

Stephanie: Hey it wasn't my fault! Your pass was too high!

Calvin: I'll say! All of Jack's passes are too high.

Coach Bill: This isn't the time to blame each other. Remember what we've talked about. What does good sportsmanship mean?

Rachel: Treating everyone the way we want to be treated.

Coach Bill: Great answer. Anyone else?

Jack: Respecting everyone whether we win or lose.

Coach Bill: Yes, another great answer. So let's be respectful and talk about how to improve in the second half.

Stephanie: That one guy on their team, number ten, is really tall. It's hard to keep him from making a basket. Can someone else come help me when he has the ball?

Coach Bill: Way to think, Stephanie! Calvin, how about when number ten has the ball, you run to help Stephanie guard him?

Calvin: Fine. But are the girls going to make any baskets? And Jack, stop going out-of-bounds! Good grief. You guys suck.

Coach Bill: Whoa, wait a minute, Calvin. That's not how we talk to each other. We're a team. If you want to be on this team, you need to support your teammates.

Calvin: I don't want to be on this team. I want to be on my old team! I want to go back to my old house in my old town! My old basketball team never lost. Everyone was awesome! I hate it here!

Narrator: Jack gently pats Calvin on the shoulder.

Jack: C'mon, man. It's not that bad here. I love living in Boomtown. Boomtown Bulldogs rock!

Narrator: Calvin shoves Jack's hand off of his shoulder.

Calvin: Boomtown Bulldogs are the worst team ever! I don't want to play anymore!

Coach Bill: All right, Calvin. This bad attitude just landed you on the bench for the second half.

Narrator: Calvin shrugs his shoulders to make it look like he doesn't care. The other players stare at Coach Bill and Calvin because no one playing for the Bulldogs has ever been benched before.

<u>Coach Bill</u>: Everyone else, listen up! This game isn't over yet! Remember when we played the Falcons and we were losing by twelve points at the half? We pulled together, made good passes and, two by two, we put points on the board. And we won! We can beat the Wildcats if we go out there and do our best. So let's go Bulldogs!

<u>Narrator</u>: *The Bulldogs walk back out onto the court. Calvin sits on the bench.*

Act II

<u>Narrator</u>: *The referee blows her whistle and the second half of the game begins.*

<u>Coach Bill</u>: Okay, Bulldogs, let's hustle out there!

<u>Narrator</u>: *The crowd cheers loudly and the players run up and down the court. Sometimes the Bulldogs make a basket and sometimes they do not. The Wildcats keep making basket after basket.*

<u>Calvin</u>: Oh c'mon, guys. Stop letting them score! Jeez!

Mrs. Peoples [looking at Calvin on the bench]: You're doing a great job, Bulldogs!

Coach Bill: Jack, watch those outside shots!

Narrator: The playing continues, and the Bulldogs fall further and further behind. A Wildcat player fouls Rachel, one of the Bulldogs. She goes to the foul line and bounces the ball, trying to focus.

Calvin: Let's do this, Rachel!

Coach Bill: Please be quiet, Calvin.

Narrator: Rachel misses the first free throw shot. Then she misses the second shot.

Calvin [yelling]: This team sucks! I'm out of here.

Narrator: Calvin stomps out of the gym and into the hallway. Calvin's parents, Mr. and Mrs. Peoples, leave the bleachers and follow Calvin into the hallway where they see him tear down a poster that was hanging on the wall.

Calvin [kicking the poster on the floor]: I hate it here!

Mr. Peoples: What's going on? This is not how you play a game, Cal! And you tore down a poster that doesn't belong to you. Not okay!

Mrs. Peoples: I know your team is losing, but this is not how you deal with it. You are twenty years old, Calvin.

Narrator: Calvin sits on the floor and taps his head lightly against the locker behind him. He does not respond to his parents.

Mr. Peoples: Are you really this angry about a basketball game? Could you be taking your anger about moving to Boomtown out on your teammates?

Mrs. Peoples: You know it takes some time to feel comfortable in a new town. It won't be long before your new basketball team will—

Calvin [interrupting his mother]: No, they'll never be like the Gators! These players are terrible. And I don't like anybody here. I miss my friends and Coach Tim. Coach Bill doesn't coach the right way. This team is going to lose every game! I want to go home to *Green Valley*. Our *real* home!

Mrs. Peoples: Well, you are right about a couple things, Calvin. This team isn't like the Gators, and Coach Bill isn't like Coach Tim. But there are things about the Bulldogs that are pretty cool, like both men and women get to play on this team.

Calvin: These girls suck at basketball.

Mrs. Peoples: Do you know that for sure? You've only been to two practices and two games. I think Stephanie made some pretty good shots in there.

Calvin: Can't we move back to Green Valley?

Mr. Peoples: No, Calvin, we're staying in Boomtown. Grandma and Grandpa are getting older, and they need our help. Uncle Peter does all he can, but his ice cream shop is the busiest place in town these days. Our family needs us, Calvin. This is where we need to be.

Mrs. Peoples: Plus, Calvin, Boomtown has so many fun things to do. Trust your dad and me. We grew up here! Wait till you see those fireworks on the Fourth of July!

Calvin: Ugh. That's so far away.

Mr. Peoples: We know it's tough to move to a new place. It's okay to be frustrated and miss your friends in Green Valley. You can always call or email them, you know? Things will get better, Cal.

Calvin: Yeah, okay.

Mr. Peoples: Now, as for your basketball team, I don't know if they will win a single game this season. How are you going to handle that?

Calvin: I don't know.

Mrs. Peoples: Why don't we talk about that on our way to Scoops? I think your coach and teammates deserve an apology, don't you?

Calvin: Yes.

Mrs. Peoples: What about the poster you tore down?

Calvin [looking down the hall where the poster was hanging]: The tape is still on the wall. I'll go hang it up.

Narrator: Calvin walks over to the space where the poster had been hanging and presses it against the tape that is on the wall. He smooths out the new wrinkles and brushes off some dirt. Mr. Peoples walks quickly into the gym to tell Coach Bill that they will meet the team at Scoops, the ice cream shop. The game is almost over.

Act III

Narrator: Calvin and his parents arrive at Scoops. Calvin's Uncle Pete, Mr. Peoples' brother, greets them happily. He can tell by the look on Calvin's face that Calvin is not happy, so he gives him a hug and tells him that a fresh batch of waffle cones will be ready for the team in a few minutes. The team walks in.

Rachel: Hi, Calvin.

Calvin: Hi.

Jack: Hi, Calvin. Why did you leave early? The game wasn't over.

Calvin: I know.

Narrator: The players and Coach Bill sit down at the table with Calvin. Mrs. Peoples carries over more chairs so everyone can sit at the same table.

Coach Bill: You played hard, everyone. I'm really proud of you. Stephanie, that was an amazing shot you made right at the end!

Stephanie: Thanks!

Calvin: Did we win?

Jack: No we lost.

Calvin: Oh.

Jack: You shouldn't walk out of a game like that, Calvin. That's not being a good team player.

Calvin: I know.

Jack: So why did you leave?

Calvin: I don't know.

Mr. Peoples: Yes you do, Calvin.

Calvin: Stop it, Dad.

Stephanie: I know why you left. You were mad because we were losing.

Narrator: Calvin nods his head. Uncle Peter comes out from the back of the ice cream shop and hands a big box to Coach Bill.

Coach Bill: Oh great! They're finally here.

Jack: What's here?

Coach Bill: Our new team T-shirts! Check them out!

Narrator: Coach Bill lifts the lid of the box and pulls out one T-shirt. Coach shows everyone the back of the T-shirt where there is a big ice cream cone and "Scoops" written in fancy letters.

Mr. Peoples: Very nice. You guys are going to look sharp in those!

Coach Bill: What do you think, everyone?

Rachel: Cool! Can I have mine?

Jack: I want mine too!

Coach Bill: All right. Let's pass them out while we wait for the waffle cones to be ready.

Narrator: Coach Bill begins to pass out the new T-shirts. The players are happy and chatting with each other. But Calvin is looking straight down at the table. Coach Bill hands Calvin his T-shirt. Calvin holds it and stares at it. Then his vision blurs with tears. He puts the T-shirt up to his face and begins crying. Everyone looks over at Calvin. He covers his face with the T-shirt as he cries.

Calvin [with a T-shirt covering his face]: I'm really sorry.

Coach Bill: Calvin, are you okay?

Calvin [lowers the T-shirt from his face]: No. I'm sorry about the game. I'm sorry to everybody. I'm just...

Narrator: Calvin begins to cry again. His face is red and he covers it with the T-shirt again.

Rachel: It's okay, Calvin. Don't cry.

Calvin: I can't help it. I can't help it! I'm sad. I miss my old team. I want to go back home. But I can't. I live here now.

Stephanie: I moved here two years ago. I don't like moving. I cried a lot when I moved. Also, I had so many boxes. I was so tired of carrying heavy boxes!

Mrs. Peoples: Yes, I'm pretty tired of carrying boxes too, Stephanie!

Narrator: Calvin uses his new T-shirt to blow his runny nose.

Rachel: Yuck, Calvin! That's your new shirt!

Calvin: Oh, right. I know. I just didn't have a tissue. Stephanie, did you miss your old friends?

Stephanie: Yes. Especially my best friend Laura. She came to visit me once though.

Calvin: Yeah, I want my friends to come visit me too. My friend Matt is really funny. He's a great basketball player. He never misses a free throw.

Jack: Never?

Calvin: Well, I mean sometimes he misses, but he's really good.

Coach Bill: You're smiling, Calvin. That's nice to see! I didn't think you knew how to smile.

Calvin: Ha, ha. You guys should see the Green Valley Gators play. No one could beat us at basketball!

Coach Bill: Hmm, you must have been pretty good. I bet if you give us a chance, the Bulldogs might surprise you. Right, everyone?

Rachel: Yeah, we creamed the Bears last month!

Jack: Remember all those rebounds I got? Just kept getting them, one after another. It was sweet.

Mrs. Peoples: Well, speaking of sweet, it looks like your cones are ready for some ice cream.

Narrator: The players line up to pick out the flavor of ice cream they want.

Coach Bill: Oh my, I think I want a scoop of all these flavors! Thank you so much for treating us, Peter.

Jack: Yes, thank you!

Stephanie: I'm going to have strawberry ice cream. It's my favorite.

Rachel: I like cookies and cream. Yum.

Narrator: Everyone sits down to eat their ice cream.

Coach Bill: Calvin, I know moving to a new town is tough. But we're glad you're here. We may not win every game, but we have a lot of fun. Remember what we talked about at halftime today. Being a good team player means respecting everyone, whether we win or lose.

Calvin: Yeah, I know. Sorry.

Coach Bill: Apology accepted. Maybe the next time we practice you can show us some of your old basketball team's winning moves?

Calvin: Don't worry. I got moves.

Mr. Peoples: Uh-oh. You asked for it!

Narrator: Calvin stands up and begins to dance with one arm in the air and one arm on his hip. His teammates cheer him on, saying, "Go Calvin, go Calvin, go Calvin!" Calvin grabs his new T-shirt and swings it in the air like a lasso. Everyone laughs.

What Do You Think?

1. Have you ever played on a team that lost? How did that feel?

2. Do you think it is better to be a good team player or a good athlete?

3. In this play, we learn that Calvin and his parents recently moved to Boomtown. Have you ever moved to a new city before? What was that like? Was it hard or easy to make new friends?

4. Is it okay to cry in public? What do you think?

Laundry

It's time to wash my clothes.
How long it's been, who knows?
It's not my favorite thing to do.
I would much rather visit the zoo!
How about you?

I have to do it today,
So might as well get it out of the way.
I let it go far too long,

Laundry

Doing that was really wrong.
Now it's going to take a lot of time,
About that I'm not feeling fine.
Would you do it for me?

Now I look for the laundry soap,
And think to myself, what a dope.
I forgot it the last time at the store.
I'm not having a good day,
LOTS to do before I can play.
Do you have any soap I can borrow?

Got the laundry started finally,
Put in the first load without a smiley.
Couldn't do much in between,
Felt like I was always at the machine.
That was the price I had to pay,
For putting my laundry on delay.
Have you ever put off doing something?
I bet you have... Was it ever laundry?

New Love, Spilt Milk, and Potbellied Pigs

So now the clothes lie on my bed,
And the hardest part is right ahead.
Sort by this and sort by that,
And I couldn't find my blue hat.
Folding the sheets is a pain in the rear.
Almost done, not to fear!
I can't wait to get this laundry done.

Laundry, laundry, go away,
Come again some other day.
Or don't come ever, as in never.
I guess that can't be the case,
It's the truth I have to face.
So laundry, laundry ever more,
Keep a knockin' at my door.

Would you mind answering the door?

What Do You Think?

1. Do you do your own laundry? What is the hardest part of doing laundry?

2. Are there other chores you dislike? If so, which ones?

3. Is there a chore that you like to do? If so, which one?

4. Is there something you usually wait to do until the last minute?

Friends
Across the Hall

The apartment across the hall from mine had been empty for over five months. I wondered who would move into the apartment. Would it be a single person or a couple, like my old neighbors? I hoped my new neighbors would be as friendly as my old neighbors. Sometimes they would invite me over for dinner, and I would bring dessert. They said the cakes and cookies I made were the best. I love to bake!

Then my neighbors told me that they were expecting a baby and needed to move to a bigger place. I was happy about their new baby, but I was sad when they moved.

I kept baking, of course. Once I tried to share some cupcakes with another neighbor down the hall. He said, "Thank you, but I cannot eat gluten." He told me that means he cannot eat things like bread, cookies, and cake. I told him I was sorry. I would be sad if I could not eat the things I bake!

One Saturday afternoon when I was just about to make sugar cookies, I heard some noise in the hallway. I looked through the peephole in my door. There were a few people carrying boxes, lamps, and furniture into the apartment across the hall. Someone was finally moving in! Right away I decided I would take my new neighbor a plate of cookies. I thought that would be a nice way to welcome him or her to the building.

I went to my kitchen and pulled out the cookie mix. I just needed eggs and oil. This was going to be easy. I mixed everything together, scooped balls of dough onto the cookie sheet, put the sheet in the oven, and set a timer for twelve minutes. I was so curious about my new neighbor. Was it a man or a woman? Old or young? Would we become friends? I hoped so.

The timer rang and I pulled the cookies out of the oven. But they were way too hot to take across the hall. I had to wait another fifteen minutes to let them cool. I am not very good at waiting. Actually, I am very *bad* at waiting. My grandma used to tell me, "Samantha, patience is a virtue." I still do not know what that means. Also, I still do not have any patience.

I tried to find something to keep me busy. But I kept going back to the peephole to watch the people carrying boxes. After a few minutes, I saw a thin woman with long hair begin to hug the other people and thank them. Then she closed the door. Hooray! My new neighbor must be the woman with long hair. *She looks very friendly*, I thought.

After the cookies cooled I put some on a plate. I decided to save the rest for my boyfriend, Collin. Collin loves to eat the things I bake, and, like I said, I love to bake. Lots of people say that we are a good match. We like a lot of the same things, like watching *Star Trek* and volunteering at the cat shelter. Collin cannot have a cat in his apartment, so he likes to play with my cat Erma when he comes over.

I got Erma from the cat shelter. If I could, I would bring home more cats from the shelter. I have talked about it with my service coordinator, Ron. He says that I do not make enough money to pay for more cat food and litter. Also, I would need to clean the litter box a lot more if I had another cat. I do not like that chore at all. I tell Erma that she is an "only cat" because she does not have a brother or sister cat. Erma does not laugh, but I do.

As I was putting plastic wrap on the plate of cookies for my new neighbor, I heard her door open and close. I ran over to the peephole and saw my new neighbor walking down the hall. Oh, shoot! Now I would have to wait even longer to meet her! I looked at Erma. "Now what are we going to do?" I asked her. She did not answer me. Instead, she walked over to me and rubbed against my leg. When she does that it means she wants me to pet her.

I spent the next forty minutes petting Erma, brushing Erma, washing the dishes I used to make cookies, and waiting to hear my new neighbor come back.

Finally, I heard the door open and close. I walked across the hall with the cookies and knocked on the door. The woman with the long hair answered the door.

"Hello," she said.

"Hello, I'm your neighbor across the hall," I said.

"It's nice to meet you. I'm Mel. It's short for Melanie. Please come in," she said.

"I'm Sam. It's short for Samantha," I said. "I made some cookies for you."

I handed her the plate and looked around inside her apartment. There were boxes everywhere. Then I saw a plastic pet carrier on the floor. The door was open.

"Do you have a cat or dog?" I asked.

"Yes, my cat Fran is somewhere in here. I just picked her up from my old apartment. And thank you so much for the cookies!" Mel said. Mel had a big smile and I liked her right away.

"I have a cat, too! Her name is Erma. Maybe our cats could meet sometime," I suggested.

"Sure, why not?" Mel said.

We talked for a few minutes about our cats. Then I asked Mel where she used to live. I told her that I had lived in my apartment for six years. I told her that I liked her cow-print rug.

"Thank you," Mel said. Then she motioned to all the boxes and said, "Well, I better start unpacking."

"Oh, okay," I said.

I was not ready to go back to my apartment. I wanted to stay and talk more. But I remembered my dad telling me that I should not "wear out my welcome." This means you can stay somewhere so long that people want you to leave. I wanted Mel to be my friend. I did not want to wear out my welcome at her apartment. So I said, "It was nice to meet you," and walked to the door.

"Thank you again for the cookies, Sam! That was so thoughtful of you," said Mel. "After I get unpacked, maybe you would like to come over for dinner sometime?" she asked.

"Yes, sure! Let me know when," I said.

I was so happy about my new neighbor. I called Collin when I got back to my apartment and told him all about Mel.

"That's great, sweetie," Collin said. "Did you say you made cookies?"

Like I said, Collin likes to eat the things I bake.

"Yes, I made cookies. What time are you coming over?" I asked him. It was Saturday. Collin and I go on a date every Saturday night. Most of the time we hang out at my apartment and watch *Star Trek* together.

Once a month, Collin's sister drives us to our favorite barbecue restaurant. Collin and I pay for our own dinners. My mom says Collin should pay for my dinner. I do not agree with her. Collin and I think it is fair if we pay for our own meals. So, that is what we do. Collin and I like to make our own choices.

Over the next few months, my new neighbor Mel and I became friends, just as I had hoped. Every other week she invited me over to her apartment for dinner. She made all kinds of meals, and I baked all kinds of desserts.

We had roast beef, potatoes, and chocolate cake; squash soup, salad, and sugar cookies; baked chicken, broccoli, and peanut butter pie.

When Mel invited me over for brunch, I did not know what to bring. I had never been to a brunch before. "What should I bring for dessert?" I asked Mel.

"How about mixed berries?" Mel suggested.

"But that is not dessert," I said.

Mel laughed. "Don't you like berries?" Mel asked.

"Sure, berries are good. But they aren't dessert. I could add ice cream and whipped cream, though. Then we will have dessert," I explained to Mel.

Mel laughed again. "Okay, berry sundaes it is! Sounds yummy," she said.

I really like Mel. She is kind to me, and I am kind to her. If she goes out of town, I check on Fran to make sure she has enough food and water. If I go out of town, she checks on Erma. I taught Mel how to make my lemon surprise cupcakes. (I cannot tell you, though; they are a surprise!)

Mel taught me how to do a dance called the electric slide. She said people always dance the electric slide at weddings. Mel loves to dance!

Our cats are not friends, however. When I brought Erma over to meet Fran, they just ignored each other. A lot of cats at the shelter are like that. They like to be alone. I guess Erma does not mind being an "only cat."

A few weeks ago, Mel got a new boyfriend. His name is Christopher. He does *not* go by "Chris" for short. Mel and Christopher met on a dating website. Mel says they are opposites. Mel is short. Christopher is tall. Mel is talkative. Christopher is quiet. Mel has a messy apartment. Christopher has a very clean house. But they both like to go running. That is what they did on their first date. Collin and I have never gone for a run together. We prefer to go on walks.

One Saturday night, Collin and I went on a double date with Mel and Christopher. Mel and I wanted to see a funny movie. Christopher wanted to see a scary movie. I do not like scary movies. They give me scary dreams.

So, we all decided to go to the funny movie. Collin and Mel and I laughed a lot. I did not hear Christopher laugh one time.

After the movie we went to dinner. While we were eating, Mel began to talk about her cousin's wedding. "It is going to be such a big wedding," she said. "Even my aunt and uncle from England are flying into town!" She seemed excited.

"The wedding is next Saturday, right?" I asked.

"Yes. Are you sure you don't mind checking on Fran?" Mel asked. Mel said she and Christopher would be gone most of the day of her cousin's wedding.

"I am happy to," I said. "I think Fran is starting to like me."

"Of course she likes you," Collin said. "Who wouldn't like you, Sam?" He held my hand and gave me a kiss on the cheek.

"I think you are right, Collin," Mel said. "Fran is a lot more comfortable with you, Sam, than she is with most people." I smiled at my boyfriend and my friend. I felt thankful for both of them.

Collin excused himself to use the restroom. I had more questions about Mel's cousin's wedding.

"How many bridesmaids are there going to be? What color are the dresses?" I asked.

"Ten bridesmaids! Can you believe it? Their dresses are black with a pink bow around the waist. The flowers are mostly pink, but I think my cousin will have all white flowers. She decided to get a DJ instead of a band. At first I wasn't sure that was the best choice, but—" Mel was still talking when Christopher cleared his throat loudly. We looked at him. He was looking down at his drink.

"Did you want to say something?" Mel asked Christopher.

"Not really," Christopher said. He looked up from his drink. "I'm just tired of talking about this wedding, that's all."

"I was answering Sam's questions, Christopher. Plus, I am excited. I'm going to see a lot of people I haven't seen in a long time. Are you not excited to meet my family?" Mel asked.

"Sure, I guess. I will just be glad when this wedding is over," said Christopher.

"It will be over in one week," Mel said. She looked away. I think her feelings were hurt. My feelings would be hurt if Collin had talked to me that way.

Just then Collin came back to the table and our food arrived. I could tell we were not going to talk about the wedding again. We ate our food and talked about the weather and Erma and Fran.

When we got back to my apartment, Collin asked, "Why did everyone get so quiet at dinner?"

"I think Mel and Christopher are mad at each other. He said something mean when you were in the restroom. He said he wanted to stop talking about her cousin's wedding. He said he wanted it to be over," I explained.

"But Mel is so excited," Collin said.

"I know. I think he hurt her feelings," I said.

"That's not good. He should be nice to his girlfriend," Collin said.

I hugged him and told him that he was right. For the second time that night, I felt very grateful for my boyfriend. I felt sorry for my friend.

A few days later, I heard a knock on my door. When I opened it, Mel was standing there. She was crying.

"I thought opposites attract," Mel said.

"What? What is wrong?" I asked.

I did not like to see my friend crying. It made me sad, too. "What is wrong?" I asked again.

"I broke up with Christopher today. I told him that I did not like the way he talked to me at dinner last Saturday night. Do you remember? He said he wanted to stop talking about the wedding," Mel said.

I nodded my head.

"Yes, I thought it was mean," I said.

"It *was* mean," Mel agreed. "It was mean and rude and thoughtless. I have heard him talk to other people that way a couple times. But I never thought he would talk to me that way."

"I'm sorry, Mel," I said. I wanted to be a good friend, so I just listened and let her talk.

"I always heard that 'opposites attract.' I thought it was good that Christopher and I were different in so many ways. I was wrong. I want a boyfriend who is kind and doesn't care about my messy apartment. I want a boyfriend who wants to meet my family. Why would I take someone like him to my cousin's wedding when he doesn't even want to hear about it?" Mel sniffed. I handed her a tissue and told her I was sorry again. "Thank you," she said.

Then she said, "I'm actually here to ask if you would want to go to the wedding with me on Saturday?"

"You want me to go with you to the wedding?" I asked. It sounded like a lot of fun. But Mel and *Christopher* were invited, not Mel and *Sam*.

"Yes, it would be great if you could come. Otherwise there will be an empty chair and a cold plate of food next to me," Mel said. "I know you and Collin usually go on a date on Saturdays, so I understand if you want to think about it."

I was already walking over to pick up my phone. "Let me call Collin," I said.

Collin answered his phone and I told him what happened. He agreed that I should go to the wedding with Mel.

"Okay, I'm in," I said to Mel as I hung up the phone. "But do you think we might be able to bring an extra piece of the wedding cake home for Collin?" I asked.

"Sure! Thank you, Sam! I'm so glad you can come," Mel said. I was happy to see that my friend was excited again. "Do you have something to wear?" she asked.

"I have a purple dress that I wore to a dance last year. Let me show it to you." I wondered if my dress would be fancy enough. This sounded like a very fancy wedding. I pulled the dress out of my closet and showed it to Mel.

"Oh, it's very pretty, Sam!" Mel said. "My dress is silver, so we will look very nice together! We are going to have a lot of fun."

Then I remembered that I was supposed to check on Fran. And now, what about Erma? "What should we do about Erma and Fran?" I asked.

"I will ask a coworker to check on them if you are comfortable with that? I trust her. She has watched Fran for me before," Mel said.

"Okay, that sounds good. I guess there is just one more thing," I said. I got up and walked over to my radio.

"What is it?" Mel asked.

"If I'm going to do the electric slide in front of all those people, I need another lesson," I said.

"You got it!" Mel said. "Sam, you are the best wedding date ever."

What Do You Think?

1. What does Sam like to do in her spare time? Do you have any hobbies you like to do in your spare time?

2. Do you live in an apartment, townhome, house, or some other kind of home? Do you know your neighbors? If so, what do you think about them?

3. Sam felt sorry for Mel when her new boyfriend was rude to her. What would you have done if you were Sam?

4. Have you been to a wedding? What was your favorite part? What was your least favorite part?

Mystery Baker

Characters

1. Frank

2. Fluffy

3. Buffy

4. BoBo

5. Willie

6. Debra

7. Mr. H

8. Narrator (The narrator tells the readers what the characters are doing. This person reads all *italicized*, or *slanted*, words.)

Narrator: This is a play, which is a story that can be acted out on stage. Before the action starts, the main character, Frank, would like to introduce himself and the other characters to you.

Frank: Hi, my name is Frank. My parents and some friends call me Frankie, but everyone else calls me Frank. I am thirty-one and I live at home with my parents. I work at a bakery called Sweety Treaty.

I am in a play called *Mystery Baker*, which you are about to read. There are seven people, or characters, in the play. Of course there is myself, Frank. My boss at the bakery is Fluffy. Fluffy owns Sweety Treaty, and she is very nice. She gave me a job when no one else would. I have worked at the bakery for three years. I mostly wash pots and pans, but sometimes I help with the baking.

Buffy is Fluffy's twin sister. She helps at the bakery when she can, but it's hard for her to lift things since she was in a car accident. Buffy teaches the flute and piano.

Debra has worked at Sweety Treaty since she graduated from high school. I don't know how old she is, but she reminds me of my mom. Debra is in charge of selling all the cookies, cakes, and breads.

BoBo and Willie are two guys who hang out at the bakery almost every day. They live nearby, and Sweety Treaty is like a second home to them. BoBo is retired, and Willie works part-time as a janitor at the high school. BoBo and Willie are funny.

Mr. H is the last character, but I can't tell you much about him. He is part of the mystery. Okay, now it's time for action!

Act I

Scene I

Narrator: *Everyone is in the back of the bakery working.*

Fluffy: Good morning, everyone. This is going to be a busy week! Remember, we have to make a ton of cookies for the Salvatore wedding.

Frank: Don't worry, Fluffy. I'm going to work very hard this week!

Fluffy: You are always a hard worker, Frank. I appreciate that. By the way, everyone, I will be gone for a few hours around lunchtime today. I have some errands to run.

Debra: Where are you going?

Fluffy: I just have some stuff to do.

Frank: What kind of stuff?

Fluffy: Just some stuff, I said. Let's get back to work. Remember, cookies, cookies, cookies! The Salvatore wedding is tomorrow.

Narrator: The bell on the front door rings.

Debra: I better go see who just came in.

BoBo: Anybody home?

Willie: Maybe they knew we were coming and ran away.

BoBo: Do you think they are hiding from us?

Debra: Morning, boys. What can I get you?

Willie: How about two black coffees for starters?

BoBo: I will take two donuts, and put them on his bill. [BoBo points at Willie]

Willie: So, what's new, Debra?

Debra [whispering]: I think Fluffy has been acting strange lately.

BoBo: What do you mean?

Debra: Shh! She's back in the kitchen. I don't want her to hear us talking about her. She is leaving the bakery a lot, and she won't talk about what she is doing. Oh, here's Buffy walking in. Let's ask her what's going on with Fluffy.

Narrator: Buffy walks in the door.

Willie: Hi, Buffy! Nice to see you. [whispering] We were just talking about Fluffy and we think something weird is going on.

<u>Buffy</u> [walks closer to the group and whispers]: Really?! I have been thinking the same thing! She seems to have a lot of secrets lately. At first, I thought she had a secret boyfriend. But she's been wearing the same stained jeans and ripped sweatshirt for days and days. She wouldn't do that if she wanted to impress a new boyfriend.

<u>BoBo</u>: Maybe Fluffy is sick and doesn't want us to find out?

<u>Debra</u>: Oh, Bernard, that's a terrible thought. Should one of us ask what is going on?

<u>BoBo</u>: I didn't think anyone around here knew my real name!

<u>Willie</u>: Bernard? Your real name is Bernard? Ha, ha!

<u>BoBo</u>: Yes, *Willard*, my name is Bernard.

<u>Willie</u>: Why do people call you BoBo?

BoBo: I used to be a clown named BoBo. I was even in the circus for a while. Hey, you know the circus is in town? Willie, you look like a clown. You should go try out!

Willie: Ha, ha. Aren't you funny? Maybe the circus is looking for a two-legged horse's ass. You would be perfect!

Debra: That's not very nice talk this early in the morning! Back to Fluffy...

BoBo: I don't think we should ask her what is going on. Instead, the next time she leaves the bakery, ask to go with her. She will have to talk about her secret then.

Willie: Hey, that's a sneaky idea.

Debra: I don't know. Maybe we are being too nosy. Let's wait a few days and see what happens.

Buffy: All right, but I'm a little worried.

Narrator: Fluffy and Frank walk to the front of the bakery carrying trays of cookies.

Debra: Has anyone been to the circus yet? It's been in town a couple of weeks already.

Willie: Hey, Frank, did you know BoBo used to be a clown? A real clown!

Frank: Yes, I know. Can you do some clown tricks, BoBo?

BoBo: Sorry, Frank, I'm retired. Wait! What's that behind your ear?

Narrator: BoBo reaches behind Frank's ear and pulls out a coin.

Frank: Good one!

Scene II

Narrator: BoBo and Willie go home. After a couple of hours, Fluffy comes back to the bakery. Frank and Debra are boxing up cookies. Buffy is sitting at a table looking at the Sweety Treaty bank account on her computer.

Frank: Hi, Fluffy. Look at all the cookies we finished for the Salvatore wedding!

Fluffy: Way to go! Thank you both for your hard work. I've been so busy with other things lately. I don't know what I'd do without you and Debra!

Buffy: A man called for you while you were out, Fluff. He had a very deep voice and said his name was Mr. H. Isn't it strange that he didn't give me his full name?

Fluffy: Mr. H. is a man I knew when I lived in New York City.

Buffy: Why haven't you talked about him before?

Narrator: The bakery phone rings.

Fluffy: I'll get it!

Narrator: Fluffy runs to her office to answer the phone.

Buffy [looking at Debra and Frank]: I'm going to say something. I'm worried. Who is this "Mr. H" person? Fluffy doesn't usually keep secrets from me. What if she's in trouble and needs our help? She can be so stubborn. Here she comes...

Narrator: Fluffy walks back into the room.

Fluffy: That was Mr. Honeywaddle. I know you're curious, Buff.

Buffy: Who in the world is Mr. *Honeywaddle*?

Fluffy: Mr. Honeywaddle is Mr. H.

Buffy: Oh. What does he want?

Fluffy: Not much. He was just calling to ask a few questions.

Buffy: Questions about what?

Fluffy: Don't worry about it, Buffy. He was just asking about things in Fairview.

Buffy: Okay, I won't worry. It still seems a little odd to me.

Frank: Does anyone want to go to the circus tonight? If we work fast we could finish the cookies and go together.

Debra: Good idea! Let's go to the circus! Do you need to ask your parents first?

Frank: No, I'm an adult and I'm my own guardian. My mom and dad like it when I go out without them. They have "date nights" when I'm not home.

Debra: Okay, great. What about you, Buffy?

Buffy: I wish I could go, but I have two flute lessons tonight. In fact, I should probably leave now.

Narrator: Buffy gathers her things and heads for the door.

Frank: Bye, Buffy. Drive carefully!

Buffy: Thanks, Frank. Goodbye, everyone!

Narrator: Frank blows some powdered sugar off the tip of his nose and takes some cookie sheets to the sink to wash them.

Fluffy: I need to run another errand in a few minutes, but maybe I'll join the two of you at the circus later. How are the cookies coming along?

Debra: I think we're in the home stretch. Once I finish these amoretti cookies, all we have left to do is coat the rest of the crescent cookies in powdered sugar.

Frank: Why does the Salvatore family need *so many* cookies? Is everyone in Fairview going to the wedding?

Fluffy: The Salvatore family is Italian, and the cookie table is a tradition at many Italian weddings. Dozens and dozens of small, fancy cookies. I think some people go to weddings just for the cookie table!

Debra: I saw a show on TV about the mob. Lots of illegal business deals happen at Italian weddings, you know. All those mobsters in one place... Maybe they send secret notes to each other in the cookies, like the fortunes in fortune cookies!

Fluffy: Debra, you know that's a stereotype. Not all Italians are in the mob!

Debra: I know, I know. Frank, do you know what the mob is? It's like a gang that does things that are against the law. But it's hard for the police to catch them because they do most of their crimes in secret.

Frank: I know what the mob is. Do you think there is a mob here in Fairview?

Debra: You never know.

<u>Fluffy</u> [rolling her eyes]: Debra, you've been watching too much TV.

<u>Debra</u>: Well, I'm just saying, you never know. Okay, Frank, let's finish up so you and I can go to the big top!

Act II

Scene I

Narrator: That night, Frank and Debra go to the circus. When Frank walks to the concession stand to buy peanuts, he sees BoBo talking to some of the circus performers. Frank walks over to them.

<u>Frank</u>: BoBo! Hi!

<u>BoBo</u>: Well hello, Frank! What a nice surprise! Let me introduce you to some of my buddies from the good old days. This is Sal, the sword swallower. This is Sofia. She is a trapeze artist. And this is Magnus, the lion tamer.

Narrator: Frank shakes hands with everyone and tells them he is glad to meet them.

BoBo: I'm going backstage to help these guys with a few things.

Frank: Cool. What are you going to do?

BoBo: Nothing too exciting. I'm just going to go stick my head in a lion's mouth.

Frank: You're funny, BoBo. Can I come?

BoBo: Sorry, Frank. Only circus performers are allowed to go backstage.

Frank: Okay. I should go back to my seat anyway. Debra will wonder where I am.

BoBo: All right, man. I'll see you soon.

Narrator: *BoBo gives Frank a friendly pat on the shoulder and then walks backstage. As Frank walks back to his seat, he runs into Fluffy. She is with a strange man.*

Fluffy: Well look who it is! Frank, good to see you.

Frank: Hi, Fluffy.

Fluffy: This is Mr. Honeywaddle. Mr. H, this is Frank.

Mr. H: It's a pleasure to meet you, Frank. Fluffy talks about you a lot. You must be a very good worker.

Frank: I love working at the bakery. I have a lot of friends there. My friend Debra is from the bakery. She brought me here tonight. We're sitting right up there.

Narrator: Frank points up to where Debra is sitting. Debra sees them and waves.

Frank: I also saw BoBo, and best of all, I got to meet some of the circus people. I met a lady who does the trapeze and the sword swallower and—

Mr. H: Did you say you met the sword swallower and a trapeze artist?

Frank: Yes, and I also met Magnus the lion tamer. I shook hands with all of them.

Fluffy: Excellent! Would you mind coming with Mr. H and me to talk about something important? And don't touch anything with that hand.

Narrator: Frank tells Debra that he is going to talk to Fluffy and Mr. H and then follows them out of the circus tent.

Scene II

Narrator: Frank, Fluffy, and Mr. H are sitting in the Sweety Treaty van. Mr. H has a small box on his lap.

Fluffy: Frank, it's very important that you don't tell anyone—not Debra, not your parents, not anyone—what we're about to talk about. Do you understand?

Frank: I understand. Don't worry, I'm good at keeping secrets. I won't tell anyone.

Fluffy: Have you noticed I've been out of the bakery a lot lately?

Frank: Yes. Everyone at the bakery thinks you've been acting weird.

Fluffy: [laughs] Well, there's a good reason for that. When I lived in New York I was a secret agent, like a police investigator, for the government. I stopped doing that kind of work when I moved to Fairview and opened the bakery. When the circus came to town a couple weeks ago, I got a call from Mr. H. He's a secret agent too.

Mr. H: I have been following this circus for the last four months. I knew someone was printing counterfeit money, or fake money, and selling it to the mob. Making counterfeit money is a serious federal crime.

Frank: Did you say "the mob"? I'm surprised there are mobsters in Fairview.

Fluffy: Yes, well there are criminals in every town. Our plan is to arrest the counterfeiters and get the money before the mob gets it. Once the mob has control of the money, it will be too tough to trace.

Frank: Who do you think is making the fake money?

Fluffy: Three nights ago, while I was watching people go in and out of the circus cars, I *think* I saw Sofia, the trapeze artist, carrying a big stack of paper. Sal the sword swallower was with her, and he was carrying a large printer. They went into a purple circus car. But it was so dark that I can't be sure it was them.

Mr. H: So, we have a test for you, Frank.

Frank: What test? I don't like tests.

Fluffy: Don't worry, all you need to do is hold out your right hand. Mr. H has a special light in that box. He's going to wave it over your hand. We'll know right away if Sal and Sofia have been making counterfeit money.

Frank: How?

Mr. H: The ink used to print money is very unique. Anyone using this ink will have traces of it, like small specks, all over their hands. If they shake hands with someone, some of the ink will rub off on the other person's hand. But you can't see it without this light. If you've got the ink on your hands, it will glow bright green.

Frank: Okay, let's do it.

Narrator: Mr. H takes the light out of the box. It is small and makes a buzzing sound. Mr. H waves the light over the palm of Frank's right hand.

Fluffy: Gotcha!

Mr. H: Do you see that, Frank? Right there between your thumb and index finger?

Frank: It's bright green. We caught them!

Narrator: Just then, Frank turns to look at a noisy group of teenagers walking into the circus tent. Mr. H is still holding the light close to Frank, and the back of Frank's shirt turns bright green.

Mr. H: Did you see that, Fluffy?

Fluffy: I sure did! Frank, will you turn around again?

Narrator: Frank turns around and Mr. H waves the light over Frank's right shoulder.

Fluffy: There's a ton of ink on your right shoulder.

Frank: Huh?

Mr. H: There's more here than on your hand. Did Sal or Sofia touch you on your shoulder?

Frank: No. But BoBo did.

Fluffy: Holy cow. BoBo's involved?!

Mr. H: He has to be. You can't get this much ink on your hands unless you've been handling money that was just printed. Your friend BoBo is up to no good.

Act III

Narrator: When the circus ends that night, Fluffy and Mr. H go backstage and arrest Sal the sword swallower and Sofia the trapeze artist. But they can't find the counterfeit money or BoBo. In the morning, Fluffy and Mr. H meet for coffee at the bakery to talk about where BoBo and the money might be.

Mr. H: Do you think BoBo has already skipped town?

Fluffy: Maybe, but his car is still in his driveway. And I know BoBo is afraid of flying. Unless he's hitchhiking, I bet he's still in Fairview.

Narrator: Debra and Buffy walk in the front door of Sweety Treaty.

Fluffy: Good morning.

Buffy: Hi, Fluff. What are you up to?

Fluffy: I'm enjoying the ambience here at Sweety Treaty. What are you doing here?

Buffy: I left my phone here yesterday and I came to get it. Debra is here to box up the cookies for the Salvatore wedding. What are *you* doing here? C'mon, Fluffy. Tell me the truth.

Narrator: Fluffy looks at Mr. H, and he nods his head. This means it is okay for Fluffy to tell Buffy and Debra about everything that happened at the circus the night before. Fluffy tells them how Frank's shirt helped them catch the criminals and discover that BoBo was part of the crime.

Debra: I just can't believe it. BoBo? But he's here almost every day, like family.

Buffy: So this is why you have been so secretive lately? And you must be Mr. H?

Narrator: Mr. H nods his head.

Fluffy: Yes, this is Mr. Honeywaddle. I'm sorry I've been so sneaky. But I couldn't say anything until we caught the counterfeiters. Although we're still looking for BoBo.

Mr. H: Don't forget the money. We're still looking for that, too.

Debra: Wow, Fluffy, I never knew you were a secret agent! Maybe I'm dreaming?

Buffy: No, Debra, you're not dreaming. Fluffy caught a lot of criminals when she lived in New York. She moved back to Fairview to live a quieter life. Fluffy, have you been in any danger?

Fluffy: Don't worry about me, Buff. I know what I'm doing. Right now we need to focus on finding BoBo.

Debra: Here comes Willie. Maybe he'll know something.

Narrator: Willie walks in the bakery. He looks upset.

Willie: Hi, guys. Has anyone seen BoBo? He called me early this morning and said he was calling to say goodbye. Why would he do that? Now I can't find him anywhere.

Fluffy: We're looking for BoBo, too. Has he done anything strange or different over the past couple weeks?

Willie: Nope. He's been the same old BoBo. Why are you looking for BoBo?

Mr. H: Are you sure? He hasn't done anything unusual?

Willie [scratching his head]: I don't know if this means anything, but yesterday morning I saw some makeup or paint on BoBo's face. I started to tease him about it. But he took a hankie out of his pocket and wiped the makeup off really fast. Then he told me not to say anything about it.

Buffy: Well, BoBo was a clown before he retired, maybe he—

Fluffy and Mr. H [at the same time, interrupting Buffy]: The circus!

Narrator: Fluffy and Mr. H jump up and head for the door.

Willie: What? What's going on?

Fluffy: We have to go to the circus right now! Debra and Buffy will fill you in.

Narrator: *Fluffy and Mr. H realize BoBo is disguised as a clown and planning to escape arrest by leaving Fairview with the circus. They drive quickly to the circus. As they get out of the car, Fluffy sees Frank's bike next to the circus tent.*

Fluffy: Stop! I think Frank is here. We need to be very careful. If BoBo has taken Frank as a hostage, I'll never forgive myself if we let anything happen to him.

Mr. H: I understand.

Narrator: *Fluffy and Mr. H. walk almost silently through the empty circus tent. They are carrying guns. Suddenly they hear some voices behind the tent, near a purple circus car. Fluffy and Mr. H. sneak behind the circus car. Fluffy hears BoBo's voice. She nods at Mr. H and they run around the car and aim their guns at BoBo.*

Mr. H: Hands up, BoBo!

Fluffy: Frank! What are you doing? Are you okay?

Narrator: Frank is standing across from BoBo, aiming a stun gun at him.

Frank: I'm okay. I already caught this bad guy.

Fluffy: What are you talking about? Why do you have a Taser?

BoBo: You're as surprised as I was.

Fluffy: Quiet, BoBo! What's going on?

Frank: I work part-time for the Fairview Police Department. I'm in the Special Crime unit. But it's a secret.

Fluffy: Why is it a secret?

Frank: I work undercover. People in Fairview know I have learning problems, so they don't think I could do something like this. That's how I find out about crimes. I was supposed to be undercover at the Salvatore wedding today, but the plan changed.

BoBo: You can say that again.

Frank: My police captain thinks the Salvatore family is selling counterfeit money to people in the mob. Then last night we found out about BoBo. I knew if I found him, I could stop him from giving the money to the Salvatores.

BoBo: And I told you where the money is. So why don't you let me go? I'll leave town with the circus and you'll never see me again.

Fluffy: No way, BoBo. You're going to jail. [turning to Frank] Where is the money? Have you seen it?

Frank: Yes. It's behind a hidden door in the circus car.

Fluffy: BoBo, why did you do this? If you needed money I would have loaned you some!

BoBo: I know, Fluff. But it wasn't about the money. I was so bored. I wanted some excitement in my life.

Frank: There are other things you can do for fun, BoBo.

Fluffy: That's right, things like working part-time for the Fairview Police Department! As usual, Frank, you've done a great job. How did you know where to find BoBo?

Frank: I know a lot of things people don't think I know. I knew BoBo used to be a clown. As soon as I woke up this morning I asked myself, "How would a clown run away from home?"

Fluffy, Mr. H, and Frank [at the same time]: The circus!

What Do You Think?

1. Were you surprised to learn about Frank's secret job?

2. Would you like to be a baker or an undercover police officer?

3. In the play, people hang out and meet their friends at Sweety Treaty. Are there places in your neighborhood where you go to hang out?

4. Do you have secrets?

Mr. Tell Everything

Joe was a kind man
who loved his friends,
but he couldn't stand
to keep his thoughts in his head.

Mr. Tell Everything

Everyone knew
if they had a secret
not to tell Joe
because he'd never keep it.

He told the whole office
when someone passed gas.
He discussed his neighbors
without being asked.

Please understand,
Joe was not mean.
He tried to keep quiet
and keep his conscience clean.

But Joe would get so excited
when he knew any fact,
that the words would pop out
before he could react.

Joe didn't like tall tales
and he never told lies.
But *new* information,
he could not disguise.

Joe's friends cared about him
and accepted his shortcoming,
although they sometimes called him
"Mr. Tell Everything."

And this was all right,
until one winter day,
Joe learned about something
he knew he shouldn't say.

He overheard Gail,
his dear old friend,
say that her marriage
was nearing the end.

Mr. Tell Everything

No one else knew yet,
and it would be cruel to talk
about Gail's situation;
Joe swore he would not.

For the whole afternoon
Joe felt ready to burst.
Concealing the secret
was a whole lot of work.

Joe was tired from effort
by the end of the day,
when his best friend Kenny
came walking his way.

Kenny asked how he was,
and Joe confided,
*"I know something big
and it's so hard to hide it."*

Joe couldn't stop talking
once he had started.
He told Kenny all
of what Gail had said.

Though Joe told just one person
whom he knew could keep quiet,
still he felt guilty—he failed
and he couldn't deny it.

Kenny tried to console him,
"It's okay, I won't repeat it."
But neither friend knew
just how bad this would get.

A coworker overheard
Joe and Kenny's chat,
and then told the whole office
about Gail's husband and all that.

When Gail came to work
on the very next day,
Joe tried to talk to her
but she said, *"Go away."*

Gail was angry at Joe
and said he had betrayed her.
She wouldn't speak to him
and Joe couldn't blame her.

Joe felt very sad
to have hurt his friend.
He wanted to make sure
it would never happen again.

He decided that he
would look for a way,
to learn self-control,
and keep his words at bay.

Joe called an old teacher
and told her his need.
He was so glad he reached her;
she sent him many things to read.

Joe learned about gossip
and why people do it.
He faced his problem head-on
and began to work through it.

Gossip happens when
we do not feel good
about ourselves or who we have been,
then we say things we never should.

Joe found other hobbies
to be excited about,
and he learned to change the subject
if gossip started to come out.

The whole office noticed
how Joe had transformed.
Even Gail was amazed,
and their friendship was reborn.

Now Joe could be trusted
to keep his friends' privacy.
"Mr. Tell Everything"
he would no longer be.

What Do You Think?

1. Is it easy or hard to keep a secret?

2. Gail was angry that Joe told Kenny about her divorce. She did not even want to speak to him. Has anyone ever shared one of your secrets? Have you ever shared someone else's secret?

3. What does it mean to gossip?

4. Joe realized that he did not want to be "Mr. Tell Everything," so he asked an old teacher for help. What could have happened if Joe did not change his ways?

Payday

It was Friday and Pat could not wait. He had been thinking about payday all week long. He thought about it almost as much as he thought about his girlfriend, Ava. It was payday.

It was hard for Pat to think about anything else. He made a list in his mind of the things he wanted to buy with the money from his paycheck. Some of the things Pat wanted to buy were:

1. Friday night pizza
2. New razor blades
3. Tickets to the movies with Ava
4. Popcorn and snacks at the movies
5. Case of diet soda
6. Groceries
7. A new video game called "Plants vs. Zombies"
8. Headphones
9. Cookie dough ice cream
10. New baseball hat

Just as Pat was about to make his list longer, his friend Miles came by Pat's work station. "Hey, Pat, have you heard the news?" Miles asked.

"No," Pat said. "What is it?"

"Well, I heard a rumor that we might not get paid today," Miles said.

Pat got upset. "Stop kidding, Miles," he said.

"No joke, my friend. Everyone is talking about it," Miles said. "If you don't believe me, there are a bunch of people in the breakroom talking about it right now."

Pat had plans for his paycheck. The thought that he might not get paid today made him feel worried. He wanted to ask other people in the breakroom if the rumor was true. So, Pat left his work station and walked quickly to the breakroom.

Miles was right about one thing. There were a lot of people in the breakroom. Pat looked around and saw his girlfriend, Ava. She was on her break and looking at her phone.

"Ava, have you heard that we might not get paid today?" Pat asked.

Ava was surprised. She said, "No one told me that. Who told you?"

"Miles said people were talking about it in the breakroom," Pat said.

"Just because Miles said it, doesn't mean it's true," Ava said. But now she was worried, too. She and Pat walked over to the other people in the breakroom. They asked if anyone had heard the rumor that they were not getting paid that day. No one had heard that.

"Do you see, Pat? It was just a rumor," Ava said. "I better get back to work now. My break is over."

Pat needed to get back to work, too. When he got back to his work station, his supervisor Mary was there, waiting for him.

"Hi, Pat," she said. "Where have you been?"

"I was in the breakroom. Miles told me that we might not get our paychecks today. He heard the rumor from people in the breakroom, so I went to find out for myself. I guess I should have asked you before I left my work station," Pat said.

"Yes, exactly," Mary said. Mary reminded Pat that there were rules at work, and Pat needed to follow those rules. They were there to keep people safe. When Pat left his work station without letting Mary know, he broke a rule. Pat apologized and agreed that he wouldn't do that again.

Pat got back to work, but it was hard for him to focus. He was upset with himself for breaking a rule. He was upset that he had let Mary down.

Pat was also upset because he still didn't know if he would get his paycheck that day. He really wanted to take Ava to the movies on Saturday night. He also wanted to order pizza that night and buy a new pair of headphones. He had plans for his paycheck. There was one hour left until lunch. *Stop worrying, man*, he thought to himself. *Just think about work.*

For the first half of the day, Pat's job was to fold cereal boxes. The factory where Pat worked made different kinds of cereal. In the part of the factory where Pat worked, they made Fruit Loops.

After lunch, Pat helped to sweep the floors and clean up around the big machines that made the Fruit Loops. Pat and his coworkers liked to joke that he was in charge of cleaning up Fruit Loop poop. This was one of Pat's favorite jokes.

Pat liked the people he worked with, especially Ava. He also liked his supervisor Mary. Mary did everything she could to help Pat do well at work. She knew that sometimes Pat got tired of folding boxes and cleaning up. She encouraged Pat to go to community college so he could get a better job within the company. "Maybe someday," Pat would say to Mary.

Pat did not like the idea of going back to school. He did not do well in school. It was difficult for him to learn, and he got very frustrated.

But Pat's job was not difficult. Even if it was sometimes boring, Pat did not mind going each day. He had a girlfriend and other friends at work and a supervisor he liked. He also had a paycheck to spend.

Finally, it was lunchtime. When Pat got to the lunchroom, he looked around for Ava. They almost always sat together in the lunchroom, which is where they had met six months earlier. They had been dating ever since. Everyone at work said that Ava and Pat made a nice couple. Ava's job at the factory was in the office. She did many different things including delivering mail, making copies, sending faxes, preparing envelopes and folders to be mailed, and shredding papers that should not be put in the trash.

While Pat waited for Ava to get to the lunchroom, he decided to ask some coworkers about the paycheck rumor. A friend at one table said he heard there was a computer problem at the company that sends the paychecks. He was worried, just like Pat.

At another table, however, people told Pat that it was just a rumor. They told him not to worry. Pat didn't know what to think or who to believe.

Pat really needed his paycheck. He didn't know how he would pay for the things he needed and wanted if he didn't get his paycheck.

Pat wished he had saved some money instead of just *thinking about* saving money. If Pat had some money in a savings account, he might not feel so worried. But Pat liked to spend his money. He liked to buy new things and go out to eat and pay for Ava's movie tickets. Then, Pat spotted Ava across the lunchroom.

"Ava!" Pat called to her. Ava heard Pat and walked over to the table where he was sitting. "Have you heard anything else about our paychecks?" he asked.

"My supervisor said there is a rumor going around, but it is only a rumor. You shouldn't worry about it," Ava said as she pulled a sandwich out of her lunch bag.

"But how will I take you to the movies tomorrow if I don't get paid? How will I buy groceries? Ava, I can't help but worry," Pat said. He hadn't even touched his lunch.

"Don't you have any groceries at home?" Ava asked.

"I do, but I don't want to eat that stuff," Pat said.

Ava thought for a moment. "I have an idea, Pat," she said. "You like to make lists. How about we make a list of things we can do that don't cost any money?"

"Like what?" Pat asked.

"Like taking a walk in the park, going to a free concert downtown, hanging out at the library, going to the art museum on the free day. There are lots of things we can do that don't cost money!" Ava said. She was pleased with her ideas.

"I guess you're right. I will start the list," Pat said. He took out his phone and opened an app that let him make lists on his phone. Together, Pat and Ava made a list of ten things they could do that wouldn't cost any money. Then it was time to go back to work.

After talking with Ava at lunch, Pat felt better. He knew there were things he could do that would not cost money. He was also finished folding boxes for the day. It was time to sweep the Fruit Loop poop. Pat liked this part of his job because he got to walk around more.

The afternoon passed by quickly. About fifteen minutes before the end of the workday, the loudspeaker came on. It was the factory manager, Brian.

"Hello, everyone, this is Brian Brown. I believe some of you have already heard that there has been a computer glitch at the company that processes our paychecks. We were hopeful that they would be able to fix the problem by the end of the day. Unfortunately, they are still working to fix the problem. This means that paychecks will be delayed until Monday morning. We are truly sorry about this. I have spoken with the company president about how we can make this up to you. She has agreed to add one hundred dollars to every person's paycheck.

"The office will remain open for an extra hour this afternoon to answer any questions you may have. I will also email any updates over the weekend. Again, we are very sorry. Thank you for your patience and understanding."

Even though he had talked with Ava about things he could do that didn't cost any money, Pat was still upset. He walked to the office to find Ava, since she usually made him feel better.

When Pat saw Ava, she was putting on her coat and looking at the line of people there to ask questions. Ava clocked out and met Pat outside the office.

"Hi," she said. "I guess this rumor was true, huh?"

"Yeah, I guess. What is everyone talking about in there?" Pat asked.

"Most of the people in there need money before Monday to pay bills or feed their families. I don't know how the company is going to help them, but they are going to try. Do you need to pay any bills before Monday?" Ava asked.

"No, I don't need to pay my rent for two more weeks. But my electric bill and water bill are due at the end of next week. I hope the paycheck company fixes the computer problem by then," Pat said and began biting his bottom lip.

Ava could tell Pat was worrying. He usually bit his bottom lip when he was worrying.

"I'm worried, too, Pat. My supervisor said that the paychecks will be here Monday morning. All we can do right now is focus on saving the money we have and try to enjoy the weekend," Ava said.

She continued, "I'm going to make spaghetti for dinner tonight if you want to come over. Then we could go for a walk in my neighborhood. What do you think?"

Ava had a very kind look on her face. She had just said that she was worried too, but she was still trying to make Pat feel better. Pat realized he had only been thinking about himself.

"That sounds great. I'll come over. And I'm sorry, Ava. Sometimes I worry about things too much," Pat said.

"It's okay. We all worry. But it doesn't help to worry about things we can't control," Ava said.

Pat nodded. They hugged, and Pat kissed Ava on the cheek. "I love you, Ava. See you tonight," Pat said.

★★★

After Ava and Pat ate dinner and washed the dishes, they went for a walk. It was a nice warm evening. A lot of Ava's neighbors were outside, too.

Ava and Pat waved to people on their porches as they walked by. They talked about more things they could do together that didn't cost any money. They turned a corner and saw a family playing basketball in their driveway.

"Hello!" Ava greeted them as she and Pat got closer.

"Ava, it's so nice to see you," a woman said.

"Pat, this is my neighbor Carol and her family. Carol, this is my boyfriend, Pat," Ava said. Then she remembered something. "Carol, don't you help people with their money?" she asked.

"I do. I'm a financial planner," Carol said. "Can I help you with something?"

"Well, not me. But maybe you can help Pat," Ava suggested. Ava looked at Pat, and he nodded his head.

They told Carol about their delayed paychecks, and Pat said he could use some help budgeting his money. Carol gave Pat her business card and told him to call her next week.

As Pat and Ava walked back to Ava's house, they talked about what he could ask Carol. When they got inside, Pat grabbed a pen and a piece of paper.

"Time for a list!" he said. "So far, here are the questions I have for Carol," he continued as he began writing.

1. Does a person need to have a lot of money for someone like you to help them?
2. What do you do with the money?

3. Do you charge a fee?

4. Can you help me with my taxes?

"Did I forget any?" Pat asked Ava.

"No, I don't think so," Ava said. "What do you think about going to the library tomorrow? I heard there is a coffee shop inside now. We could hang out there and check out some books and DVDs," Ava said.

"Sure," Pat said. "I'm in." The couple kissed goodbye and Pat went home. As Pat walked home from his bus stop, he decided to send Ava an email. She had been such a big help to him that day. He wanted her to know that he appreciated her.

When Pat turned on his computer and opened his email account, he saw an email with the subject: "Update on Paychecks." He opened the email. It was from Brian, the factory manager. The computer problem was fixed. Everyone would have their paychecks on Monday morning, along with an extra $100 to make up for the inconvenience.

Pat was so relieved. Then he started to think about what he could buy with the extra $100. Maybe he could buy *two* new baseball hats instead of just one? Then he shook his head. "Come on, Pat!" he said to himself. "What are you thinking? You need to save that money, man."

He started typing an email to Ava. He thanked her for helping him. He told her that she made him happy. Then he realized he could make another list. At the top of this list, Pat typed "Things I Learned Today."

1. It doesn't help to worry about things I can't control.
2. Sometimes I only think about myself. Other people have problems, too.
3. I need to start saving money.
4. There are a lot of fun things to do that don't cost any money.
5. I have the best girlfriend in the world.

He sent the email to Ava and turned off his computer. Pat went to bed and started another list in his mind: "Important People in my Life."

What Do You Think?

1. Who would be on your list of important people?

2. Have you ever heard a rumor? Have you ever started a rumor or helped to spread one?

3. What do you do when you hear something that may—or may not—be true?

4. Pat and Ava thought of some things they could do that were fun and free. What are some *other* things you can do that are fun and free?

5. Is it easy or hard to save money?

Princess Freedom: An Update

Freedom is a wonder dog. We first wrote about her in our last book, *Lucky Dogs, Lost Hats, and Dating Don'ts* in a story called "A Day of Kindness." Freedom was rescued by her owner, Lou, when she was two years old. Four months later, Freedom was hit by a car. She was bleeding and hurt badly. But before Lou could get to her, Freedom ran away.

Lou could not find Freedom. Neighbors helped him look, but no one could find her. Then, someone told Lou that he should call the dog warden for help. The dog warden told Lou the most unexpected thing. There was a report of a dog that had run to the hospital emergency room. Somehow, Freedom knew that she should go to the hospital. And, somehow, she found it!

After the wonderful staff at the emergency room made sure Freedom was stable, she and Lou got a ride to the university veterinary hospital from a kind police officer. Freedom had serious injuries, but she got the help she needed and recovered after a few weeks. At first, nobody believed Lou when he told this story. But it was true.

Freedom is still living a great life with Lou. She is treated like a royal princess, with monthly visits to the spa. She even has her own sofa and TV! Freedom loves to go on walks. She and Lou start each day with a half-hour walk at 5:00 a.m. But this is just one of many walks she gets each day.

Lou takes great pride in how much Freedom is loved by his friends, family, and people in the community. Lou's father loves Freedom as if she were his granddaughter. He often sends her cards and homemade biscuits. Freedom gets her very own birthday cake and celebration each year.

Lou said, "For eight years she has brought so much joy to others, and that makes me very happy." Lou was also pleased to know that Freedom's story had been shared with so many people who read the *Lucky Dogs* book.

Lou talks about how he has reached the "trifecta of dog ownership." (A *trifecta* is what you call three wins in a row.) Lou said this means that Freedom has never done any of the following three things in his house:

1. Freedom has never peed in Lou's house.
2. Freedom has never pooped in Lou's house.
3. Freedom has never chewed on anything in Lou's house.

It is rare for a dog not to have done at least one of those things at one time or another. But not Freedom. She is treated like a princess, and she behaves like one, too.

One time, when Lou returned from a trip, he took a limo home from the airport. Freedom was staying with the vet, like she always does whenever Lou goes out of town. Since Lou knows the limo driver, he asked if they could stop along the way to pick up Freedom. The limo driver agreed and drove to the vet's office. Some of the employees in the vet's office saw the limo parked outside. They wondered who would take a limo to the vet. When Lou walked inside, the employees smiled. "Is that limo for Freedom?" one person asked.

Lou took a moment and finally replied, "Of course, nothing but the best for my princess."

What Do You Think?

1. Do you have a pet?

2. If so, tell us about your pet.

3. If not, have you ever wanted to have a pet?

4. Freedom was one of the "lucky dogs" we wrote about in *Lucky Dogs, Lost Hats, and Dating Don'ts*. What do you think makes Freedom a lucky dog?

5. Have you ever taken a ride inside a limo? What was it like?

Spilt Milk

It happened fast. One moment I was walking quickly around the park. The next moment I was on the ground, looking up at the sky.

I was also in pain. I tried to get up on my own, but I felt shooting pain in my lower back and other places in my body. I decided to lie still. I worried about what would happen if no one walked by. "Help!" I yelled. No one heard me. I think I was on the ground for about five minutes, but it felt like an hour.

Finally, I heard a voice say, "Are you okay?" It sounded like an older woman.

I felt like saying, "Does it *look* like I am okay?" but that would not have been polite. I also needed this person's help. So I said, "No, I don't think so."

"Just try to relax, dear," the woman said. "I need to walk to my car to get my phone and call nine-one-one. Lie still. I'll be right back."

Who was this person? How long would it take her to walk to her car? What did I do to my back? I had a lot of questions going through my mind. I tried to breathe deeply and relax. I looked at some birds on a nearby tree. They looked so happy and pain-free. I wished I was one of those birds.

After a few minutes, the woman came back. "I called the ambulance. They will be here soon. Where does it hurt?" she asked.

"My lower back and backside. My head and arm, too," I said. "Thank you for helping me."

"You're quite welcome," the woman said. "I'm going to put my sweatshirt on top of you." She took off her sweatshirt and laid it over my chest and arms.

"What is your name, dear?" she asked.

"Mary Poppins," I said.

The woman laughed and said, "Okay, Mary, that's fine. You don't have to tell me your name. My name is Edith. You poor thing. It looks like you slipped on this muddy patch next to the path…"

Edith kept talking, but all I could think was, *I can't believe I fell again*. Leave it to me to find the one slippery spot on a paved walking path. I tend to have accidents when I'm not paying attention.

My mom used to tell me to slow down and pay attention all the time. So did my doctor, Dr. Hill. When I was about seven years old, my mom and Dr. Hill told me I had something called ADHD. It stands for Attention Deficit Hyperactivity Disorder. It is hard for me to focus. I make mistakes I wouldn't make if I was paying attention. I also need to move around a lot. I took medication when I was growing up, but it made it hard for me to sleep. So, when I turned eighteen, Dr. Hill and I made a plan for me to gradually quit taking the medicine.

Since then, I have learned to live with ADHD. It is still hard for me to concentrate. I get distracted very easily. Sometimes I switch topics in the middle of a sentence! This is just part of who I am. I stay very physically active, which helps.

"Here they come," Edith said. I heard the sirens, too.

"Thank goodness," I said. "Edith, I can't thank you enough for your help. Also, I'm not Mary Poppins, as you know. I'm Hope Allen."

Edith laughed again. "It's okay. You don't have to tell me your name," she said.

"No, really, I'm Hope Allen," I told her.

I watched Edith's face. At first, she looked doubtful. Then she looked at me more closely. Her eyes got very wide and her jaw dropped when she realized that I was telling the truth.

"Oh my goodness, you *are* Hope Allen! Wait until my neighbor Sally hears about this! She will be so jealous that I got to meet a movie star," Edith said with a very quiet giggle. "I can't wait to see your new movie, *Martina*! I'm a big fan of hers." Edith shook her head and said, "My neighbor Sally is going to be so upset she didn't come for a walk with me today!"

"If you give me your address, I will send you a thank-you card. I can send something to Sally, too," I offered.

Edith waved her hand like she was swatting a fly and said, "Oh, sweetie, there is no need for that. Besides, I don't have a pen." A moment later, she stood up and said, "Oh good, here are the paramedics."

I couldn't see them yet, but I could hear them wheeling a stretcher down the walking path.

"We're so glad you're here," Edith said. Then she whispered, "It's Hope Allen! You know, from the movies!" It wasn't a very good whisper, though, since I could hear what she said.

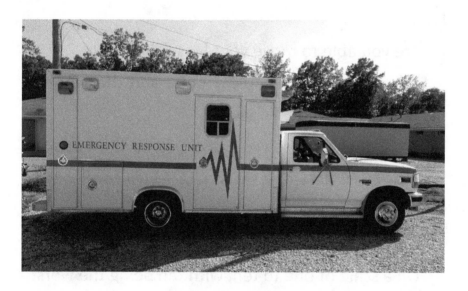

In a louder voice, Edith said, "She seems to have hurt her lower back, as well as her head and arm."

"Ma'am, we're going to take very good care of you," a man said, and he kneeled down beside me. The other man talked with Edith and made some quick notes.

The man next to me checked my pulse and said, "My name is Ryan, and that's Steve. And you're Hope, right?"

"Yes," I said.

"Have you tried to sit up yet?" he asked.

"Once, but it really hurt. I thought I should lie still," I replied.

"Are you able to move your legs?" he asked.

I took a breath, closed my eyes, and then moved my feet and bent my knees.

"Okay, that's good. We'll take you to the hospital, and they will do some tests. Just try to relax," Ryan told me.

I nodded my head.

"On a scale of one to ten, with ten being the worst, how bad is your pain right now?" he asked.

"Eleven," I said.

Yes, I can be dramatic. I'm an actress, after all. But I really was in a lot of pain.

The stretcher was lowered down next to where I was lying. Ryan and Steve lifted me onto the stretcher. Ryan gently removed Edith's sweatshirt and handed it back to her. I thanked Edith again. She nodded and said, "Get well soon, honey."

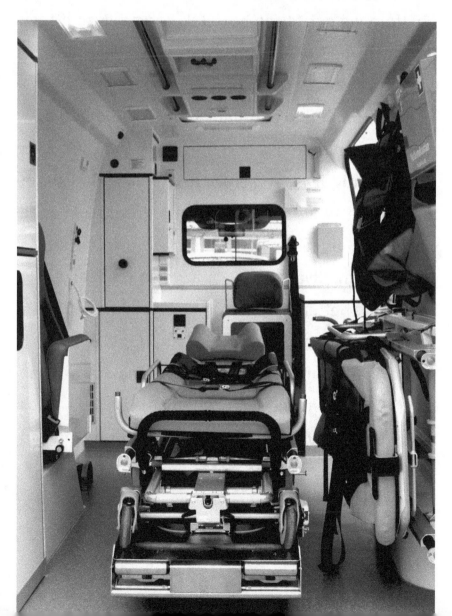

I don't remember much of the ride to the hospital, except for the loud sirens. Ryan stayed in the back with me. He checked my blood pressure. He said things to comfort me, but I could hardly hear him over the sound of the sirens.

Before we got to the hospital, I asked Ryan if they could take me somewhere private when we got to the emergency room. "It's best if the newspapers and TV reporters don't find out that I'm here," I shouted over the sirens, which really hurt my head.

Apparently, Ryan and Steve had already thought of this. "Steve has already called the hospital. They're waiting for us, and they'll take you directly into a private room," Ryan said. "Don't worry about anything but feeling better."

"Thanks, you guys. I appreciate it," I told Ryan.

Like the paramedics, the nurses and staff in the emergency room were very good at their jobs. I was taken to a private room where everyone moved quickly around me. I felt a lot of poking and prodding.

I tried to listen to the nurses who were telling me what they were doing, but I was distracted by all the other sounds in the room. There was another conversation going on, a machine that made a clicking noise, an announcement on the loudspeaker, and lots of shoes squeaking on the floor.

A man who looked younger than me walked over to me and said, "Ms. Allen, I'm Dr. Waters. Can you tell me what happened?"

"I was power walking at the park. I was rehearsing lines for a movie and doing some arm exercises. The next thing I remember, I was on my back. The woman who found me said she thought I slipped in some mud," I told the doctor. Walking, rehearsing lines, and doing arm exercises, all at the same time... That sounds like me.

"So, you don't remember falling?" Dr. Waters asked.

"No, I guess I don't. Do you think I have a concussion?" I asked.

"More than likely." Dr. Waters took something that looked like a small flashlight out of his pocket and said, "I'm going to shine this in your eyes. When I move my finger, try to follow it with your eyes." I watched him move his finger up and down and back and forth. Then he asked me to move my arms and legs so he could test my strength and reflexes. My arm still hurt, but not as much as my back and head.

Dr. Waters ordered some tests and X-rays. His voice was kind and deep. A nurse was typing at a computer, and all the sounds made me feel very sleepy.

I closed my eyes for a moment and thought how nice it would feel to fall asleep.

"Ms. Allen, we have to ask you to stay awake for a while," one of the nurses said. I opened my eyes.

"Oh, that's right. You shouldn't sleep after a concussion," I remembered. "Darn. I would love a nap right now." I smiled at the nurse. She smiled back.

"We're going to keep you busy for the next couple hours with some X-rays and other tests. We will let you sleep eventually," she said with a wink. She attached a cold pack to my head and put one under my backside. She said the cold would help reduce any swelling. I looked at her name tag, which said "Emily."

"Thank you, Emily," I said. From there I was taken to the person who did X-rays. Then I was put in a different room, and new nurses came in and out. I also got a new doctor, Dr. Cobb. She was a very short woman with a scratchy voice. She reminded me of my favorite aunt, so I liked her right away. After a couple hours, Dr. Cobb came into my room with the results of the tests.

She looked at my chart, then pulled up a chair and sat next to me. "It looks like you fell on your tailbone and broke it in at least one place. You also have a concussion and some swelling on your head. You must have fallen all the way back and hit your head on the pavement after landing on your backside. You also have some cuts and bruises on your right elbow, which tells us you probably tried to stop your fall with your right arm," Dr. Cobb said. She took a breath and asked, "Any questions so far?"

"So...I broke my butt?" I said.

I couldn't help but laugh.

"Well, yes, you broke your tailbone," she said.

I had more questions.

"How do you treat a broken tailbone? How long does that take to heal? And my head is killing me. Will you be giving me any medicine for the pain?" I asked.

"Yes, we'll give you ibuprofen soon. That will help with the pain in your head and tailbone," Dr. Cobb said.

Dr. Cobb continued, "As for healing time, you need to rest your body and your mind for at least one week to let your brain recover from the concussion."

"Oh boy," I said. "I'm supposed to be learning my lines for a new movie. That takes a lot of concentration, which is hard for me to begin with! I better call my manager so he can tell the movie director. What about my tailbone, how long does that take to heal?"

"It usually takes anywhere from eight to twelve weeks for a broken tailbone to heal. It may be painful to sit down for a while. You may want to get a donut to sit on while you heal," Dr. Cobb said. She opened a cabinet in the room and pulled out a "donut" to show me. It looked like a small round tube, like some people use in a pool.

"I am supposed to go to the opening night of a new movie in three weeks. Will I be able to go?" I asked. I thought about what the magazines would say if missed the opening night of my new move, *Martina*. This was a movie about the famous tennis star Martina Navratilova, and she was going to be there, too!

"More than likely you will feel well enough to go to your movie opening," Dr. Cobb said. She continued, "We would like to keep you overnight though, to make sure the place where you hit your head doesn't continue to swell."

"Okay," I said. "I need to make some phone calls, then."

Dr. Cobb left and I made a few phone calls. First, I called my manager, Lucas. He was kind, and told me not to worry about memorizing my movie lines until my head was better. He did laugh, however, when I told him I broke my butt. I laughed, too.

I also called my mother.

"Hope, you worry me. Please try to pay more attention when you are walking," my mom said. I told her that I would. We talked for a while. My mom said she would go to my house to let my dog out that night and again in the morning. Someone walked in my room with a tray of food and I said goodbye to my mom. I didn't realize how hungry I was until I smelled the food.

I had never eaten hospital food before. Most people say it isn't very good. But I was really hungry, and the chicken, mashed potatoes, and peas on the plate in front of me looked delicious. There was also a chocolate chip cookie and a glass of milk.

While I was eating, a nurse named Leticia came into the room to change the cold packs on my head and under my tailbone. After Leticia changed the cold pack on my head, she helped me lean slowly to one side so she could change the pack under my tailbone. While she was doing this, I was eating my mashed potatoes with one hand and scrolling through my phone with the other hand.

Just as Leticia said, "All finished," I heard a clank. Somehow, I knocked over my glass of milk. At that moment, I felt all of the worry of the day and regret for not being more careful. I couldn't believe I had just knocked over my milk. I began to cry.

"I'm sorry, Leticia," I said as I sniffled. "It has been a rotten day."

"No need to apologize, Ms. Allen. You are allowed to cry," Leticia said. She put her hand on my shoulder.

"Please, call me Hope," I said as I took a tissue from Leticia. She seemed to pull it out of nowhere. "Thank you," I told her. "I'll be okay."

Leticia smiled and said, "Yes, of course you will."

She walked around my hospital bed and began to wipe up the milk that was now on the floor. Then she looked up at me.

"When I moved to America ten years ago, one of the things people told me was that I shouldn't cry over spilt milk," Leticia said.

We laughed together. I was crying over spilt milk! Well, not really. I was crying about the events of the whole day. But it was a good joke, and it helped me feel better.

"I didn't understand what that meant at first, but I do now," Leticia said. She finished wiping up the milk and washed her hands.

"I used to be sad about things that happened, things that were in the past. Then I realized that there was nothing I could do to change those things. They were 'spilt milk,' and the best thing I could do was to learn from them and move on," Leticia said. "Oh, but you don't need me to lecture you about such—"

"No, this is helpful! Thank you. I needed that reminder," I told her.

After I finished my dinner, I was ready for bed. I fell asleep quickly. But because I had a concussion, a nurse woke me up every hour that night to make sure I was okay. The next morning, my manager picked me up at the hospital and took me home. He stayed with me that day, and woke me up when I tried to take a nap.

"Lucas, I don't think I can stay awake any longer," I told him.

"Okay, let's chat then. Tell me what happened yesterday!" Lucas said. He sat next to me and listened as I told him all about the day.

"Well, thank goodness Edith went out for a walk!" Lucas said.

"Yes, thank goodness for Edith," I said. "I wish I could send her a thank-you card or gift. I didn't get her last name, though. I have no idea how to find her."

"Hmm." Lucas was thinking. "I wonder if the paramedics wrote down her name and phone number."

"Oh, you are so smart, Lucas," I said. "Would you be able to help me find the paramedics? Their names are Ryan and Steve. I don't know their last names, either."

"I bet we can find them. Let me work on that. You should focus on resting your knocked head and broken butt," Lucas said, and then he smiled. I had a feeling my broken butt was going to be a popular joke with Lucas for a while.

★★★

In the days to come, I began to feel better. My head stopped throbbing. The cuts and bruises on my arm didn't hurt anymore. However, my tailbone was still very sore. I got used to carrying around the donut and sitting down very slowly.

A week later, Lucas found the paramedics, Ryan and Steve. I was so happy to find out that they did write down Edith's name and phone number.

I thought about what I could send her to show her how thankful I was for her help.

Perhaps a lovely flower arrangement? Hmm, not very creative. What about a box of fancy cupcakes? But what if Edith doesn't eat sugar? Then I had the best idea.

I called Lucas and told him my idea. He thought it was great, and he said he would take care of the details. I thanked him and thought for a minute about how lucky I was to have Lucas and my mother and other people in my life who helped me.

***

On the opening night of my movie, *Martina*, I was feeling great. My stylist came over after breakfast with my dress and everything she needed to do my hair and makeup. It takes a long time to get ready to walk down a red carpet.

The limo picked Lucas and me up right on time. As we pulled into the driveway of the pretty little brick house, I was surprised to see that he was as excited as I was.

The limo driver walked to the front door and knocked. Edith opened the door and walked out. She looked lovely. She was wearing a beautiful black dress and carried a tiny, black sequined purse. She looked a bit nervous, so I opened the door and got out to greet her.

"Oh, Edith, I'm so happy that Lucas found you! I'm so happy you could join me for the opening night of the movie!" I said, and then we gave each other a big hug.

"Ms. Allen, it is—" Edith began.

"You must call me Hope. If you are going to be my date, you have to call me by my first name," I told her. That seemed to help Edith relax.

"All right then, Hope, I should tell you that I have never been to a movie opening before. You will have to tell me what to do," Edith said.

"Don't worry about a thing, Edith," I said as we got into the limo.

On our way to the theater, I learned about Edith's family and her former career as a gym teacher. She also told me she used to play tennis in high school and college.

"You played tennis? How exciting! I can't wait to introduce you to Martina!" A few minutes later, we pulled up to the theater. The limo driver opened our door, and the flash of a hundred cameras greeted us.

What Do You Think?

1. If you could meet any famous person in the world, who would you want to meet?

2. Have you ever had to ride in an ambulance? If so, what was it like?

3. ADHD made it difficult for Hope to sit still and pay attention for long periods of time. Have you heard of ADHD? Do you know anyone with ADHD?

4. When someone does something really nice for you, how do you let them know you are thankful?

The Amazing Tito

Tito lifted the lid of the large trunk. Inside were all the supplies and props he needed for his magic show. He was nervous. He was about to perform his first magic show in front of a real audience.

Growing up, Tito would practice magic in front of a make-believe audience. He would pretend that he heard people clapping and cheering. He would take a bow and say, "Thank you so much! Oh, you are too kind!" He imagined thrilling people with his magic.

Now, when he imagined standing in front of an audience, his mouth got dry and his hands started to sweat. Some people are not afraid to speak or perform in front of other people. Tito wished he could be like those people. For Tito, the thought of going on stage in front of other people made his knees wobbly and his heart race. Tito had stage fright.

If only Tito could get over his stage fright, he could quit his job at the pizza shop and do magic full-time.

Tito loved magic. He loved the mystery and surprise of magic. He loved his memories of practicing magic tricks with his father. The day Tito's father made Carl, the family's pet pigeon, disappear and then reappear was the day that Tito got hooked on magic.

Tito spent a lot of his spare time and money at Faye's Fantastic Magic Shop. Faye was a good friend. She owned the local magic shop and helped Tito learn the more difficult magic tricks. Tito wasn't nervous to perform in front of Faye or his best friend, Donny. He knew Faye and Donny well. He trusted that they would not make fun of him if he made a mistake.

One day at the magic shop, Faye showed Tito a clever new trick using a coin. Later that night, Tito took a coin out of his pocket and began to practice the trick during a break at the pizza shop. While he was practicing, Tito's coworker Paula walked by and saw him make the coin disappear.

"Wow! How did you do that, Tito?" Paula asked.

"I can't tell you that," Tito said with a smile. "It's magic!"

"I didn't know you did magic. That's really cool," Paula said.

"Thanks, Paula! Magic is my favorite hobby. Well, I guess you could say it's my passion. I wish it could be my job," Tito said.

"I know what you mean. I love to paint, but I have never made any money doing it. So, I work here to earn a paycheck, and I paint for fun," Paula said. She began to walk away, but suddenly stopped.

"I have an idea! My son Diego is going to turn six next month. We're having a big birthday party for him. You could put on a magic show for the kids! I will pay you for your time. What do you think?"

Paula was very excited about her idea, but Tito wasn't so sure.

"Gosh, I don't know. I've never done magic in front of an audience before. I get too nervous," Tito told Paula.

"Don't be silly! It will be a group of six-year-olds. They will love it!" Paula said.

Tito knew that she was just trying to encourage him. He thought she would stop if she knew how bad his stage fright was. But he wasn't sure how much he wanted to share.

"I'm not sure. I can't—I mean, I don't know if I would be any good," Tito said.

Paula continued to urge Tito. "Oh, c'mon, Tito. Please say you will do it."

"Okay, okay. I'll do it," Tito said.

"Qué bueno! Diego is going to be so happy!" Paula said.

As he drove home from work that night, Tito wished he would have said no to Paula. He already had butterflies in his stomach. This was going to be a huge challenge. But Tito knew he could not get over his fear of performing in front of people if he never tried it. Tito also knew he needed help. He called his friend Donny.

"Hey, man, I was wondering if you could help me with something," Tito said.

"You got it, bro," Donny said. "What do you need?"

Tito told Donny about his conversation with Paula at work. "I have one month before the show, and I'm already nervous," Tito said. "I have read everything I can find about how to overcome stage fright, especially right before the show."

"What are you supposed to do?" Donny asked.

"On the day of the show, I'm supposed to avoid caffeine, get some exercise, and get to the show early. Then I'm supposed to relax my mind and body."

"How do you do that?" Donny asked.

"A lot of people suggest meditation. You get really quiet and focus your thoughts on one thing. It seems a little strange to me, but I don't think it will hurt to try it. Deep breathing exercises are also supposed to help," Tito said. "But before all of that, the most important thing I need to do is practice. That's where you come in..."

"I can be your audience while you practice," Donny offered.

"That's exactly what I was hoping," Tito said.

"Tito, you've been doing magic since we were kids. You got this, bro!" Donny said.

"Thanks, man. I needed that." Tito felt better after he talked to Donny.

Over the next few weeks, Tito practiced his magic show in front of Donny over and over again. Donny's favorite tricks were the card tricks. Every time Tito showed him the right card, Donny would shake his head and say, "Wow! How did you do that?"

By the day of the birthday party, Tito was ready. In the morning he went for a long walk. He left early for the party so he wouldn't feel rushed. He even felt a little excited as he walked to the front door of his coworker Paula's house.

Tito put down his large trunk of magic supplies and knocked on the door. A little boy in a pointy party hat opened the door.

"Hi! Are you the birthday boy, Diego?" Tito asked.

"No, he's in there," the little boy said, and then he opened the door all the way. Tito looked inside and saw all the people who were there for the party. He was surprised to see so many people. All of a sudden, Tito felt dizzy.

"Are you going to come in?" the little boy asked.

Tito wanted to turn around and run away. But instead, he nodded his head, picked up his trunk, and stepped inside.

"Tito! Welcome!" Paula shouted over the noise of all the people in the house. "Can I get you anything to eat or drink?"

"Water would be great," Tito shouted back as he put down his trunk. Tito felt overwhelmed, but he tried to smile and look friendly. *Just breathe, man*, he told himself.

Paula came back with a bottle of water. "I thought it would be nice to have the magic show on the back porch. As you can tell, it's a zoo in here!" Paula said loudly and motioned for Tito to follow her.

Tito picked up his trunk again and followed Paula to the brick porch at the back of her house. There was a piñata in the shape of a horse hanging from a tree branch, and a table covered in birthday gifts. Paula and Tito talked about where Tito would stand and where the kids would sit for the show. It was quiet on the porch, so they didn't have to shout at one another.

"The kids are so excited," Paula said. "We will be ready for the show in about fifteen minutes. Is that all right?"

"Sure," Tito said.

"You are welcome to wait out here or inside," Paula told Tito.

"I think I'll wait out here," Tito said.

"Okay, we'll see you soon," Paula said. She slid open the glass door and stepped back inside.

Tito could hear children laughing and squealing. Everyone seemed to be having a good time. Except for Tito. He was nervous.

He lifted the lid of his trunk to make sure he had all the supplies he needed. Silk scarf? Check. Bucket? Check. Deck of cards? Check.

He decided to do some breathing exercises to calm down. He inhaled for four seconds, held his breath for four seconds, exhaled for four seconds, and rested for four seconds.

Tito repeated this many times. He felt a little better. Next, Tito began to meditate. He closed his eyes and imagined being in a place that made him happy— Faye's Fantastic Magic Shop. He felt even calmer. Then he went back to the breathing exercises.

Several minutes later, Tito looked at his watch. Just a couple minutes until showtime. Tito walked over to the glass door and looked at his reflection. He smoothed his hair and straightened his lucky blue bowtie. He walked back to the corner of the porch where he was going to perform and did one more round of deep breathing.

A moment later, the door slid open and children rushed outside. Paula showed them where to sit, and one by one, they sat down and began staring at Tito. The adults followed the children and stood in a group behind them.

Tito's knees felt wobbly and his palms began to sweat. He reminded himself to smile. Paula walked around the seated children and stood next to Tito.

"Children, you are in for a treat today. *The Amazing Tito* is here!" Paula said and began clapping.

Everyone else clapped, and one of the kids put two fingers in his mouth and whistled loudly.

Tito wished Paula hadn't called him the *Amazing* Tito. What if he wasn't amazing? It didn't matter now. It was showtime. Tito cleared his throat.

"Hello, everyone!" Tito said. "I have some super cool magic tricks to show you today. Are you ready?"

All the children cheered.

Tito's heart was pounding. He turned to get his magic hat out of the trunk and start the show. He took one step and his foot tripped over a brick that had come loose on the ground. With his arms flying wildly, Tito fell.

Luckily, his large trunk of magic supplies was there to catch him. Tito landed inside the trunk with his legs in the air. Instantly, the children howled with laughter. The adults were laughing, too.

Tito was stunned. Here he was, at the start of his first magic show, wedged inside his own trunk. It was so silly; Tito couldn't help but laugh, too. He could never have done this trick if he had tried!

When he struggled to get out of the trunk, everyone, including Tito, laughed even harder. He stood up and straightened his bowtie.

Then, Tito realized he wasn't nervous anymore. In fact, he was having fun! A good laugh was exactly what he needed.

"All right, which one of you pushed me?" Tito asked, and the audience giggled. He saw Paula standing at the back of the porch, giving him the thumbs-up sign. For the very first time, Tito felt confident in front of a crowd.

He walked slowly to his trunk, grabbed a handle, and dragged the trunk closer to where he was standing. "Let's try this again!"

That day, Tito became *The Amazing Tito*.

What Do You Think?

1. Have you ever had to talk or perform in front of a group of people? Were you nervous? What helps you relax?

2. At first, Tito did not want to do a magic show for Diego's birthday party. But Paula kept asking, so Tito agreed. What do you think about this? Have you ever said yes to something you didn't really want to do?

3. What are your hobbies? Do you do one of those hobbies as a job?

4. Tito was finally able to relax when he had a good laugh. Who do you laugh with the most? Do you have a favorite funny memory?

Thoughts of a Writer

Once there was a cow who could only say meow.

*How would you feel if you were a cow
and could only say meow?*

What would you do?

The other cows would not be able to understand you.

Maybe you could go to live with cats.

What do you think about that?

If you lived with cats you might feel out of place.

Maybe you could paint your face?

But the cats might know you are a cow,
even if you could say meow.

My name is Lou. How are you? No, I am just kidding. My name is really Alice. A lot of people just call me "Al." I am twenty-five years old, and I live on Long Island. It is just outside New York City. I like to write. I also like to think. For me, thinking is relaxing. I wrote about the meow cow. I'm not sure why I did. It just came to me. The meow cow doesn't fit in. Not with the cows and not with the cats. Sometimes I don't feel like I fit in. I wonder if you have ever felt that way. Do you meow when others moo? Maybe you do.

Some people think I am funny. I like to tell jokes. Here are a few of my jokes:

What did the modern-day reindeer say to Santa Claus?
Let's get going, big boy, and don't forget your cell phone.

What is orange, red, and white all over?
Nothing I can think of.

What do a tuna fish sandwich and pork fried rice have in common?
You can't get them at Wendy's.

Two women were talking. Then they kept talking and talking and talking. Two men were talking and then they stopped. A spy wasn't talking. A dog couldn't talk.

The wheels on the bus go round and round. They also fall off sometimes.

The doctor told me I owed her money. I said I would pay her when I got better.

I hope you liked my jokes. People tell me that I like my jokes more than they do. What do you think? Were they funny? Do you think your jokes are funnier?

I like to laugh at myself sometimes, even when no one is around. It is usually because I did something silly. One time I could not find my glasses. I looked everywhere. I even worried about having to buy a new pair of glasses. Then I felt something funny on my head as I sat down to eat dinner. Sure enough, there were my glasses. Ha!

One morning I got dressed for work in the dark because the electricity had gone out. When I got to work, I looked down at my feet. I was wearing one black shoe and one brown shoe. They were the same kind of shoes, but different colors. No one seemed to notice I was wearing mismatched shoes. But I had a really good laugh!

Would you like to hear the poem I made up while walking down the street yesterday? I'll tell it to you, but first I want to tell you about my friend Alvin. Most people call him "Al," too.

I met Al in the sixth grade, and we became close friends. We were a couple of Als running around Brooklyn, making up songs, and telling silly jokes.

Then Al's family moved to Dallas before tenth grade. We promised each other that we would keep in touch, but we didn't. I guess that just happens sometimes.

About a month ago, I was in my favorite bookstore in Brooklyn when someone bumped into me. I turned around, and there was Al! He was a lot taller, but I recognized his big brown eyes and sweet smile right away. We were so excited to see each other. We made plans to meet two days later for coffee.

We had so much to talk about that afternoon over coffee. Al said he had moved back to Brooklyn a year ago. His father needed help taking care of his mother, who had cancer.

"I'm so sorry to hear that," I said.

"Thank you. She's feeling much better now," Al said. "You will have to come over for a visit. They will be so excited to see you! Now, tell me what is going on in your life."

I told Al about my family and my ex-boyfriend and how much I hated my job as a server at a fancy restaurant. Al was a great listener. He asked me good questions like, "Al, if you could have a job doing anything, what would it be?"

"Oh, that's easy," I said. "I would be a writer."

"Well then, you should be a writer," Al said.

"It isn't that easy, you know." I started to tell him all the reasons why it is hard to become a successful writer. But he didn't want to hear them. He said I should just start writing. He also suggested I look for a new job to pay the bills until I could make money from writing. I thought about it for a moment, and decided I agreed with Al.

Al looked down at his watch and said suddenly, "I've got to go! I'm so sorry. I lost track of time. I'm supposed to meet a friend for dinner. But let's get together again!"

"You bet," I said. "I'll text you." Al gave me a hug goodbye and rushed out of the coffee shop.

I pulled out my laptop and stared at a blank screen for a long while. No ideas that day. Sometimes they call that "writer's block." Instead of getting frustrated, I started searching online for a new job.

I looked at a lot of different jobs. I wasn't interested in most of them. Other jobs were either too far away or required education I didn't have. Then I saw an ad for a dog-walking service called "Happy Tails." I thought the name was clever, so I was interested right away.

Happy Tails was busier than ever and was looking for dog walkers. I called the number on the ad. I spoke with a very nice woman who emailed me an application. Two days later, I was a dog walker for Happy Tails!

I kept my job at the restaurant for a couple more weeks, just to make sure I could make enough money at Happy Tails to pay my bills. There were lots of dogs to walk, so it didn't take long before I could quit my job at the restaurant.

I walk dogs for rich people and not-so-rich people. I walk friendly dogs and scared dogs. I walk big dogs and small dogs. One dog I walk is a cute little pug named Pete. His owners do not have children, and they treat Pete like their baby. He is a friendly and funny dog. He loves attention and makes little snorting noises when people pet him. On one of our walks, I came up with a poem about Pete and gave it to his owners.

> Each day, I can't wait to walk Pete.
> He's so jolly, cute and sweet.
> Pete is such a special dog,
> I write about him on my blog.

If I could, I would walk him for free,

I wouldn't ask you to pay me.

But I can't afford to do that...

And now Pete is chasing after a cat!

Another dog I walk is a large black poodle named Fifi. Fifi's owner Gloria is also a dog groomer, so Fifi always looks her best. I think Fifi knows she is a pretty girl. She prances when she walks and seems to like wearing all the sparkly collars and hair bows that Gloria puts on her.

One of my favorite Happy Tails clients is the owner of three frisky terriers, Lonny, Larry and Lulu. Their owner says they are the smartest dogs he's ever owned. Sometimes I'm not so sure how smart they are, but Lonny, Larry and Lulu are a lot of fun. I walk them at the same time, and we take up a lot of space on the sidewalk!

During my first few weeks as a dog walker, I got a lot of exercise and met a lot of people who stopped to pet the dogs. I also thought a lot about Al.

Al and I had always gotten along so well. He really seemed to care about me. Also, I loved his big brown eyes. I decided I would call him and ask him out on a date; not a chat over coffee, but a real date. The more I thought about the idea, the more excited I got. Besides, I wanted to let him know how happy I was in my new job.

One day, when I was walking the three terriers, I started to think about what I would say to Al when I called.

Hi, Al! It's Al. Have you ever been on a date with someone named Al?

What do you think about going on a date? I think it would be great!

I just bought a new dress. How about I take you out to dinner so you can see how pretty I look in it?

I was rehearsing how I would ask Al on a date when the dogs and I ended up behind a couple walking very slowly. The two men did not seem to be in a hurry to get to wherever they were walking. They held hands and strolled down the middle of the sidewalk. They looked happy just being together.

I thought this was nice, but I had more dogs to walk after Lonny, Larry and Lulu. I cleared my throat and said politely, "Excuse me, would you mind if we walked around you?"

One guy looked back at me and said, "Sure! Go ahead."

The man and his boyfriend moved over to the right so I could walk past.

When the dogs and I were in front of them, I turned around and said, "Thank you."

One of the guys was tall with light blue eyes. The other guy had big brown eyes, just like Al's. It took me a second, but then I realized it *was* Al.

Al and I looked at each other. I was surprised. When Al and I met at the coffee shop a few weeks earlier, he didn't tell me that he had a boyfriend. I had no idea that he was gay. I had just been thinking about how I would ask him out on a date! The thought actually made me laugh, so I decided to tell him.

"Al!" I said with a smile. "Do you know that I was just thinking about asking you out on a date? I guess that would have been a bad idea!" I walked up to Al and we gave each other a big hug.

"Hey, Al," he said. He put his hands on my shoulders and gave me a warm smile. "This is my boyfriend, Charles. Charles, this is Alice, my friend from childhood I was telling you about."

Charles and I shook hands. "So nice to meet you," he said.

"You too," I said. Then I looked at Al. "You didn't tell me you had a boyfriend, Al. You were about to get asked out on a date by a woman who wants to show off a new dress!" I made a joke because that is what I usually do when I feel uncomfortable. I wasn't uncomfortable that Al was gay. However, I was a little sad that my friend didn't choose to share this part of his life with me when we met a few weeks earlier. Of course, it was his business to share. I just wished he would have decided to share it with me.

"I was going to tell you. But then I had to leave quickly because I was late, remember?" Al said. "Anyway, we've been dating for five months."

"Six months," Charles corrected.

"I guess you are right!" Al said. He and Charles looked at each other and grinned.

I was happy for them. I wanted to get to know my friend's boyfriend.

"That's awesome. What do you think about meeting up for drinks sometime? There's a new—" Just then, Lonny and Lulu began to wrestle with each other. Their leashes got tangled, and all of a sudden there was a swirling ball of terriers barking and rolling around on the sidewalk.

I bent down and tried to untangle the dogs and leashes. "Larry! Stop barking! Lonny, do not bite your sister!" When the dogs finally calmed down, I looked at Al and Charles. They were laughing. We must have caused quite a commotion.

"They are feisty little ones!" I said, and I laughed too.

"Well, Al, you didn't tell me that you had three dogs!" Al said.

"Oh, they're not mine. But I wanted to tell you that I took your advice and got another job while I work on my writing career. I'm now one of the most popular dog walkers for Happy Tails," I said.

"Congratulations!" Al said.

Al and Charles bent down and gave the dogs a few pats on the head and scratches behind the ears.

"Charles loves dogs," Al said.

"Oh yeah?" I said to Charles.

"They are the best," Charles said. "Dogs are better than people. I'd rather spend time with my dogs than anyone."

"Excuse me?" Al said, looking at Charles.

Charles smiled. "Except for you, sweetie, of course," he said.

I checked my watch. "I need to get going. Fifi the poodle is waiting," I said. "I was going to ask, though, if you two want to get together sometime at the new wine bar. It's around the corner from where we had coffee, Al."

"That sounds great," Al said.

"Yes, I've actually been there. The food is delicious," Charles said.

"Okay, good! Al, I'll text you and we will set a date," I said. "See you later!"

"See you later!" Al said.

"Nice to meet you," Charles said.

"Same here," I said. Lonny, Larry, Lulu and I walked away. All of a sudden, I felt the urge to write. It is hard to write while walking dogs, so I began talking to the dogs.

Once there was a girl named Alice,

She did not live in a palace.

Her job was to walk dogs,

It was better than walking hogs.

Maybe not...

Maybe it would be fun to walk hogs.

Alice learned something new today,

Her friend Alvin is gay.

He will not be her next date,

Romance will have to wait.

Or maybe there is someone for her,

Soon, Alice may meet a fine sir.

How nice that would be...

What Do You Think?

1. How would you finish this poem?

2. Have other people thought you were funny?

3. Do you ever get silly?

4. What would it be like to be a dog walker?

What's up with the Potbellied Pig?

Claire and Jim had been married for a year. As soon as they got married, they began talking about getting a dog. While growing up, Jim volunteered in an animal shelter. He knew there were lots of dogs in shelters that needed good homes, so he and Claire decided to adopt a dog from a shelter. When the day to choose a dog arrived, Claire and Jim walked cheerfully to the local animal shelter.

"What a lovely day," said Claire. "Maybe we can take our new dog to the park later?"

"Sure," Jim replied. "I wonder what kind of dog we're going to find. Don't you think a little wiener dog would be great? I'd love a lap dog to keep me company when I'm working at home."

"You mean a dachshund? I suppose that would be nice. But I think a Lab would be fun. They love to play and be around people," said Claire.

Jim and Claire agreed that the most important thing was that their new dog be a friendly dog. They planned to take their dog to the park, the farmers' market, and their favorite coffee shop where they allowed dogs on the patio. They wanted a social dog to join their family.

When they got to the animal shelter, there were not as many animals as they expected. A volunteer named Pete told them that the shelter had had a very successful adoption fair last weekend. Many dogs and cats had been adopted. Now the shelter had room to take in more animals that needed homes.

Pete told Claire and Jim that there were still a few cats and dogs, as well as some smaller animals, like rabbits.

Jim was disappointed. "Do you think we should come back another time?" he asked Claire.

"Let's take a look around while we are here," said Claire. "You never know what we might find." She smiled at Jim, and they walked toward the animal cages.

Claire liked watching the kittens play in their cages. But since she was allergic to cats, they moved on. They walked past a few dogs that didn't seem very friendly. Claire and Jim felt sorry for those dogs. But none of them seemed like the right dog for them.

Suddenly they heard a strange sound mixed in with the barking and howling. It didn't sound like a dog or a cat. It was a squealing sound coming from the far end of the room. Claire and Jim passed a few empty cages before arriving at the source of the noise. In the last cage was a small, darkly colored pig.

She began running back and forth, wagging her little curly tail and grunting. The tag on her cage said, "Potbellied Pig: Lily." Jim began laughing and looked at Claire, who had a big smile on her face. "What's up with the potbellied pig?" he asked.

"I don't know. But isn't she the cutest thing?" replied Claire. "Look at her. She's so excited. I swear she's even smiling! Let's ask if we can play with her."

Jim and Claire found Pete, the volunteer who greeted them when they arrived at the shelter. They asked if they could spend some time with Lily. Pete put a leash on Lily and they all walked into a small room with chairs and animal toys. Right away, Pete took a seat on the floor and began petting Lily.

"Lily is a potbellied pig. This means she will stay smaller than a regular pig, but she could still grow to over one hundred pounds. Her former owner didn't realize how big she could get. The woman's landlord didn't allow pets over fifty pounds. So she gave her to us and asked us to find a good home for her," Pete explained.

"She's nearly sixty pounds. Though she doesn't look that big, does she?" Pete asked.

"No, I guess not," said Jim. "Our rental lease doesn't say anything about a weight limit for pets. Dogs *or* *pigs*," Jim laughed and looked at Claire. "Are we really thinking about adopting a *pig*?"

Claire shrugged. She was still smiling. "Maybe," she said. "What else can you tell us about potbellied pigs?" she asked Pete.

"Well, Lily is our shelter's first potbellied pig. We know that pigs are very smart. They can learn tricks, but they are very stubborn. They don't do anything they don't want to do. Here, we printed some basic health information and feeding suggestions," Pete said as he handed Claire a piece of paper.

Jim and Claire had a lot of fun playing with Lily. The shelter worker said they could take her outside in a grassy fenced-off area behind the shelter. When she wasn't getting a back scratch, she rooted with her nose on the ground.

When Jim called her name, she scurried over and looked up at him. Her little curly tail wagged. She wasn't the dog that Claire and Jim had expected to adopt, but Lily was winning them over. At one point, Lily rolled over onto her back, inviting someone to give her a belly rub. Jim laughed and bent down to rub the pig's belly.

"Did someone teach you this trick, Lily?" Jim asked. "It's a good one, yes it is. Yes, and you are a sweet girl..." Jim went on to babble and talk to Lily like she was a baby.

"I think someone might have made a new friend," Claire said to Pete. "That's the voice Jim uses when he talks to dogs he likes." Jim just smiled and kept petting Lily.

Still, Claire and Jim knew it would be foolish to adopt Lily without knowing if they could care for her. They needed to think this over.

Eventually, they thanked Pete for his help and told him that they might be back. Pete gave them another piece of paper that explained the process of adopting animals from the shelter. He invited them to come back and visit Lily again.

At first, Jim and Claire were quiet as they walked away from the shelter. Finally, Claire said, "I hate to leave her there."

"I know. She's such a friendly little pig. Does that paper from the shelter say anything about where a pig likes to sleep? Would she even want to sleep inside?" Pete asked.

Claire shook her head. "There really isn't much on here," said Claire as she looked at the paper. She and Jim wondered if it would be hard to find a vet to treat Lily. They wondered just how stubborn pigs really were. They wondered if they could afford to feed a pig. When they got home, Claire decided to call her sister for advice.

At first, Claire's sister thought she was kidding. When she realized Claire was serious, Claire's sister asked, "Why on earth would you want a pig? They're dirty! And your neighbors will think you've absolutely lost it!" This was not the reaction Claire had been hoping for.

Jim called his father for advice. Jim's father liked to give advice. He had lived on a farm when he was a young boy. Jim thought he might know something about pigs.

After Jim told him about Lily, Jim's dad said, "I like pigs as much as anybody. Who doesn't love a nice crispy piece of bacon?" Jim's dad also liked to crack jokes. "But seriously, why would you want a pig in your house?"

Claire and Jim felt discouraged. Their family didn't seem to think it was a good idea to adopt a pig. But Claire and Jim kept thinking about how lovable Lily had been.

The next evening, Jim and Claire went to the library to research potbellied pigs. Claire checked out one book about pigs in general and another book about potbellies. Jim looked up information on the computer. There were a lot of websites and groups for people who have pigs as pets. Jim also found the phone number for a local vet who treated farm animals.

When the librarian at the checkout counter saw Claire's books, she said, "I grew up on a farm. We always had pigs, and I loved them."

"Cool! We're thinking about adopting a potbellied pig," Claire told the librarian.

"How wonderful! You know, they're not actually dirty animals. They just have a bad reputation because they use mud to cool themselves down," said the librarian. Claire was happy that someone finally had something positive to say about owning a pig.

When the couple got home, they decided to make a list of pros and cons. The "pros," or reasons it would be a good idea to adopt a pig, were very encouraging.

The books from the library described pigs as social, affectionate animals. They like to be around people. They are clean and don't shed. They only need yearly vet visits as long as they're well cared for. They are smart and can be trained easily. They like to go on walks. They like to cuddle.

"Sounds like the perfect pet to me," said Jim.

"On the other hand," said Claire, "this book says pigs are clever and manipulative, especially when it comes to food. They will even open the refrigerator!" Claire read more from the book. "If they don't get enough attention and outdoor time, they can become bored and destructive. They use their noses to root in the ground, so they will mess up the yard. Their lungs and bodies are easily stressed by overheating and bad weather. It also says that pigs can be aggressive, like dogs, if they don't have a good leader," Claire said. "Hmm. So we will have to pig-proof the kitchen, keep her out of the sun, and learn to be good pig leaders."

"I think the backyard would be a fine place for Lily," Jim said as he walked to the couple's office and returned with a copy of their lease agreement. "Just as I thought, our lease doesn't include anything about a weight limit for pets. Though, we should still double-check with Mr. Parker, especially since he planted all that new grass last year," said Jim. Claire agreed that they should talk with their landlord.

Claire and Jim learned other things from their research at the library. Providing a good living space for a pig was more involved than either of them had imagined. They would need to make sure that their yard had the right amount of shade, shelter, rooting space, and a cooling mudhole or shallow pool. That was just the outside. This was becoming a difficult decision.

***

The next morning on her way to work, Claire stopped to visit Lily. When Claire called her name, Lily ran right over to her feet and wagged her curly tail.

At dinner that night, Claire told Jim how sweet Lily had been that morning. "I'm almost certain she remembered me," Claire said.

"You know, when I was looking online for info about pigs, I found a place called Red Gate Farm. It's a working farm that also offers tours for 'city folk' who want to know more about life in the country. Tomorrow is Saturday. Why don't we go check it out? The pigs on the farm may not be potbellies, but it would still be helpful to see them in their natural habitat," Jim said.

"You know me. I'm always up for an adventure," said Claire. "Let's do it."

The next morning, Jim and Claire drove out to the farm. They watched as the city thinned out into suburbs. After a half hour, they passed Claire's office building. "I'm happy I'm not going there today," Claire remarked as they passed the exit she usually took.

As they continued to drive, the houses grew more and more sparse, until only fields of corn and other crops could be seen from the road.

After an hour of driving and listening to the GPS on Claire's phone, they spotted the red gate that gave the farm its name. They drove in slowly and parked their car in one of the spaces reserved for guests. A friendly older couple walked over to greet them.

"Welcome! I'm Donna and this is my husband, George. Our son Andy will be showing you around. He's just over there," Donna motioned to a man standing near the large barn. "You can pay him, and he'll give you the grand tour. Enjoy!"

Jim and Claire were pleased to see that they were the only ones there, which meant that they would have a private tour. They walked over to Andy, handed him twenty dollars, and introduced themselves. "Welcome to Red Gate!" said Andy with a smile. "I'm happy to show you folks around."

Although they were mainly there to see the pigs, Claire and Jim were also excited to meet the other animals. They saw cows that had just finished milking and been put out to graze. There were chickens running around and squawking.

"That's my sister Molly," said Andy, as he pointed to a girl bent over, putting eggs in a basket.

Claire burst out laughing. "I didn't see her at first, so I thought you were calling one of the chickens your sister!"

"Oh, that's funny," said Andy. "Animals do start to feel like family though." The tour continued. Andy showed them the goats, ducks, and a new baby lamb and the lamb's mother.

"How precious," Claire said. "Maybe we should adopt a lamb too."

"How about one farm animal at a time?" Jim said.

"What kind of animal are you folks getting?" asked Andy.

Jim and Claire told him about their visit to the shelter and how they had become smitten with a potbellied pig named Lily.

"Pigs do have *a lot* of personality," Andy agreed.

He finally led them to the pig pen. "Oh wow, they're huge!" exclaimed Jim.

These pigs were much bigger than Lily. Each had to weigh hundreds of pounds. Some looked like they were over a thousand pounds.

There were pigs rolling in mud, pigs rooting around in the ground, and even a pig rolling an old soccer ball around with its snout. The pig pen was quite large. It had a roof and a gate that opened to a pasture. Claire noticed a heavy padlock on the gate and asked Andy about it.

Andy chuckled. "Gertie, the happy girl rolling in the mud over there, figured out how to push the latch open. They're smart devils," he said. "They'll get into anything and everything. I've never had a potbelly. But a pig is a pig. I suggest child locks on everything in your kitchen."

"Yes, we've read that," Claire said. "Any other tips for pig-proofing a house?" Before Andy could answer, one of the pigs walked up to him and nuzzled the side of his blue jeans. Andy bent down and petted the pig.

"This is Sal. He just loves to be with people," Andy said. He invited Jim and Claire to pet Sal.

"What a lovable guy," Claire said. She smiled at Jim, and Jim smiled back.

"Like I said, they feel like members of the family." Andy looked around at all the friendly farm animals. "I'm going to miss them when I leave for veterinary school in a couple weeks," said Andy.

"Oh? Congratulations! Where will you be studying?" asked Jim.

"I got into Ohio State, which means I'll be moving up north. It'll be the first time I've been away from the farm. I built my own house on the property a few years ago, just on the other side of those pines," Andy said, pointing to a group of very tall pine trees.

"I'm sure your animals will miss you too," said Claire.

Andy smiled.

"I suppose so. I plan to move back here after I finish school. There's only one vet in our town, and she's going to retire in a few years. The plan is for me to take over her practice. Now I'm just looking for someone to rent my house. The extra money will help while I'm in school."

"Sounds like you've got a good plan. Best of luck to you," said Jim.

"Thanks very much. I appreciate that," Andy said.

Jim looked at his watch. "Oh my goodness, it's already noon. We should get going," he said to Claire.

Jim looked back at Andy and said, "Thank you so much for the grand tour."

"Yes, it was great. You and your family were so kind. Maybe we can bring Lily to meet Sal and Gertie sometime," said Claire.

"Sure thing. You folks take care," Andy said. Claire and Jim shook Andy's hand and walked back to their car. By the time they reached the red gate at the end of the driveway, Claire and Jim agreed that Lily the potbellied pig should come to live with them.

Right away, Claire called the shelter to say that she and Jim wanted to adopt Lily. It was Pete, the volunteer who had helped them earlier that week, who answered the phone.

"Oh, that's great!" said Pete. "You can stop by whenever you like to fill out the application." Claire told him they would be there soon.

Pete greeted them when they walked into the shelter. Claire filled out the application. Pete looked it over and said that they should be able to pick up Lily as early as Tuesday afternoon. Jim and Claire asked if they could see Lily while they were there. Pete said that she was enjoying some time outside at the moment.

"Would you like me to bring her inside?" he asked.

"No, I don't want to take away from her time outside. What do you think, Claire?" Jim asked.

"Let's let her have fun outside. We'll see her soon enough! Will you give this to her, though?" asked Claire.

She handed Pete a handkerchief from her purse. "I read somewhere that it can help an animal adjust more quickly to a new home if they have something with their new owner's scent. That way, we'll seem familiar to her."

"You're right about that. I'll give this to Lily," Pete said. Claire and Jim said goodbye to Pete and happily walked to their car.

***

Jim and Claire were very excited. They spent the rest of the weekend talking about how much fun they were going to have with Lily. They went to three different pet stores to buy food and toys and other supplies. They bought child locks for the kitchen cabinets and installed them. They were ready.

On Monday morning, Jim called their landlord, Mr. Parker, to tell him about their plans to adopt a potbellied pig.

"You want a *pig*?" said Mr. Parker. His tone of voice wasn't very friendly. "I don't think that's a good idea. They are messy, you know."

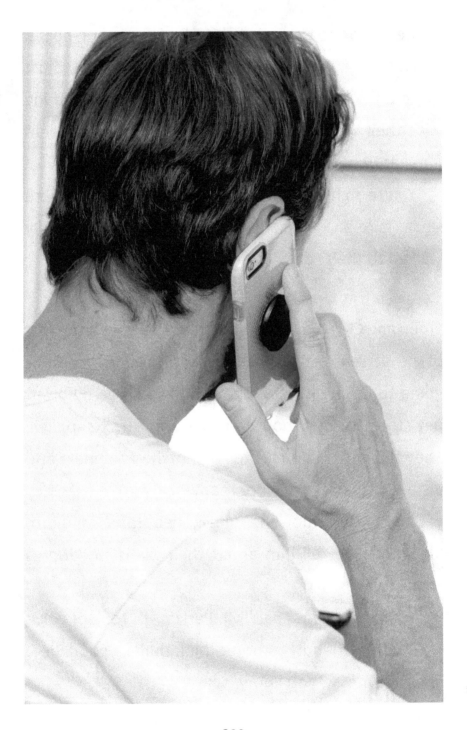

"Actually, that's not true. They are cleaner than we think. They only roll in mud to cool down," Jim said. "We'll keep her in the backyard where the neighbors won't see the mud pit."

"You want to put a mud pit in the backyard? That's new grass, you know," Mr. Parker said. Jim could tell that his landlord didn't like this idea.

"Yes, we know. We'll replace all the grass in the backyard before we move," said Jim.

"Why would you need to replace *all* the grass?" Mr. Parker asked.

"Well, because pigs need to root and that usually tears up the ground," said Jim. He added quickly, "She's not a normal-size pig, though. She's a potbelly. She'll stay small."

"How big is she?"

"She's about sixty pounds. She'll get to one hundred pounds, tops."

"I'm sorry, Jim. A one-hundred-pound pig tearing up the entire backyard after we did all that landscaping... and a mud pit? I'm afraid I'm going to have to say no," said the landlord.

Jim was shocked. He tried to convince the landlord to give Lily a chance. He promised that he and Claire would return the yard to "pre-pig" condition before they moved. He even asked the landlord if he would take a day to rethink his decision. But Mr. Parker only reminded Jim that their lease stated that the landlord had the right to "deny occupancy to potentially dangerous or destructive animals."

Jim didn't remember reading that part when he checked the lease a couple days ago. He picked up the lease that lay on his desk. There it was. "Property owner reserves the right to deny occupancy..." Jim's heart sank. He quickly ended the phone call with Mr. Parker.

He and Claire had been so excited about adopting Lily. Now it wasn't going to happen. He wondered how he would tell Claire. He decided to wait until she got home from work. He didn't want to upset her while she was at work or driving home. But when Claire walked in the door, all he could think to do was blurt it out.

"Mr. Parker said 'no' to Lily."

"You're kidding me, right?" Claire said. Jim shook his head and told her that Mr. Parker thought a pig would cause too much damage to the backyard.

Claire dropped her purse on the kitchen counter. "But you told him we would replant the grass! Why does he care what it looks like while we're here?"

"I don't know. I guess he has a high opinion of his landscaping. Or he just thinks a pig would wreck the place. Really, it doesn't matter why. This is his property, and according to the lease, he has the right to deny our request," Jim said.

He felt defeated and sad.

Claire felt angry. "What a jerk! We've been here two years and haven't given him any trouble. We pay our rent on time and even mow that stupid grass. We should move," she said. Jim shrugged his shoulders and got up to walk into the kitchen. He opened the dishwasher and began to slowly put away the dishes. Claire picked up the lease. She noticed that it was nearly time for them to renew their lease for another year.

"Wait. Wait! I have an idea," said Claire. She walked into the kitchen. Jim turned around to see that Claire was grinning.

"Am I supposed to guess?" asked Jim.

"I have three words for you. Red. Gate. Farm. Remember? Andy is going to vet school and needs renters for his house. Our lease is up in a couple weeks."

Claire held up the lease. "You work from home. My office is almost as far from here as it is from the farm." The more Claire talked, the more excited she was about the idea. "Well, Jim? What do you think?"

Jim took a minute to think. Then he said, "I think it's worth a shot." As soon as the words were out of his mouth, Claire gave him a big hug and a kiss. "So, I guess we should call Andy now," Jim suggested.

"I'm on it!" exclaimed Claire. She looked for the number to Red Gate Farm on her phone and called. Andy's mother Donna answered. Claire asked to speak with Andy.

"I'm sorry, he's over at his own place. Packing up boxes. Did he tell you folks he was moving? All the way up to Columbus. Going to vet school. Leaving us here with an empty house to look after. Molly—that's our daughter—is so sad. Oh, I'm sorry to trouble you. We're gonna miss him, that's all," Donna said. Claire liked Donna. She seemed so familiar, even though they had just met a couple days ago.

"Yes, of course you are going to miss him. Andy told us about his upcoming move when we were at your farm on Saturday. My husband and I would like to talk with him about possibly renting his house. Would you mind giving me Andy's phone number?" Claire asked.

"Oh heavens, wouldn't that be nice!" Donna exclaimed. She gave Claire Andy's phone number. Claire called him right away.

"Hello, Andy, this is Claire. My husband Jim and I toured your farm last Saturday morning."

"Oh sure. What can I do for you?" asked Andy.

Claire put her phone on speaker so Jim could join the conversation. After about ten minutes and a lot of questions and answers, Jim and Claire had a plan—a plan that would allow them to adopt Lily after all.

Two Months Later

Claire turned into the driveway of Red Gate Farm, and then took a left turn toward the small, sturdy home that Andy had built. Jim was in the garage breaking down cardboard boxes.

"Hi, honey," Jim said as Claire got out of her car. "I think this is the last of the boxes. Who knew we had so much stuff?" He shook his head, picked up the pile of cardboard, and walked over to a green recycling bin.

Claire met him at the bin and opened the lid. After Jim put the cardboard in the bin, Claire gave him a kiss.

"Well, how did it go with Lily today?" Claire asked.

"George said that Lily and Gertie were doing what all pigs do. Newcomers want to know which pig is 'top pig' in the family. Lily wanted to lie in Gertie's favorite spot, and that's why they fought," Jim said.

"I remember reading that pigs would fight for territory. I just didn't think *Lily* would fight. She is such a happy girl. Is Gertie's leg okay?" asked Claire.

"Yes, she's fine. George and Donna say thanks for the 'apology cookies' you baked, but not to worry about it. George said it isn't the first squabble on the farm and it won't be the last," Jim said, trying to imitate George's gruff voice. "Apparently, Gertie and Rupert really got into it once."

"I assume Gertie won?"

Jim nodded his head yes. "Gertie is 'top pig' at Red Gate, that's for sure."

"Did Lily seem happy? Did you spend some time with her?" asked Claire.

"Yes and yes," answered Jim with a smile. "I walked over after my conference call this morning. Donna insisted I sit for a cup of coffee and a cookie, and then I went to the pen. Lily came right over to me, wagging her curly little tail."

"Aww, I love that pig. I think I'll take her some ice cream tonight," said Claire. She and Jim walked slowly toward the house and began climbing the front porch steps.

"Isn't it awesome? In two months' time, Lily goes from being a shelter animal to living on a farm with all the love and attention she could want. Not to mention ice cream," Jim said.

"I know. I'm so happy we moved here," said Claire. When they got to the top of the steps, Claire stopped and looked around. She and Jim especially loved the view from the front porch. Claire smiled and took a big whiff of air. Quickly, she plugged her nose. "Whoa, is that fresh manure on the field?!"

"I think so. I must be getting used to it. I hardly notice it," said Jim. "However, I did notice a smell when I walked back into the house today." Jim looked at Claire, and she rolled her eyes.

"Again? Gosh, I never thought that house training a puppy would be so hard. I'm glad Andy has hardwood floors!" said Claire. She opened the front door and a small, brownish-red dachshund ran to greet her.

"Hello, Penny! I heard you had another accident today. Maybe you should go live with Lily in the pig pen? Would you like that?" Claire teased the puppy and bent down to pet her. Penny rolled over for a belly rub.

"Oh, a belly rub? You think you deserve a belly rub?" Claire said, as she happily stroked Penny's belly. "Did Lily teach you that trick? She used the belly rub trick on Jim when we met her at the shelter," Claire said and then winked at Jim.

Jim laughed and sat on the floor next to Claire. The couple played for a long time with Penny and her favorite stuffed octopus toy.

Jim told Claire more farm stories that George had shared with him that morning. Claire suggested they skip dinner and go straight for ice cream with Lily, and Jim agreed. Who knew that a potbellied pig could make their family so happy?

What Do You Think?

1. Have you ever had a pet? If so, what kind of pet did you have? What did you have to learn to be able to take care of it?

2. If not, what kind of pet would you like to have? Would you be willing to move in order to have this pet?

3. What do you think it would be like to have a potbellied pig?

4. Have you ever visited a farm? What was it like?

About the Authors

Dr. Tom Fish was Director of Social Work at The Ohio State University Nisonger Center on Excellence in Developmental Disabilities for most of his professional career. Tom is founder of the Next Chapter Book Club and has been a tireless advocate for people with intellectual and developmental disabilities and their families. As a teacher, researcher, and clinician, Tom has always emphasized the values of respect and dignity. He has focused on helping to level the playing field for people with disabilities so that they could display their strengths and be able to live the lives of their choosing.

Tom has three amazing children (Matt, Lauren, and Roger), two fantastic daughters-in-law, two darling grandchildren, and a beloved partner, Lyna. Sorry, no family pet at the moment. He enjoys swimming, playing the ukulele and coming up with new jokes—all of which are terrific of course.

Jillian Ober is Program Manager at The Ohio State University Nisonger Center, where she has worked since 2004 to promote community inclusion and social connections for people with disabilities. Among these programs is the Next Chapter Book Club, a widely-successful, community-based book club program for people with intellectual and developmental disabilities. Jillian received both her undergraduate and graduate degrees from The Ohio State University. She is an avid reader, proud aunt, and dog lover who owns (and loves) a cat.

CPSIA information can be obtained
at www.ICGtesting.com
Printed in the USA
BVHW070247110920
588362BV00005B/57